War of Hearts

USA TODAY BESTSELLING AUTHOR
TAYA RUNE

Cover Design: Sweet 15 Designs

For information contact : purplerealmpublishing@gmail.com

ISBN: 978-1-922604-29-3 (ebook)

ISBN : 978-1-922604-24-8 (paperback)

ISBN : 978-1-922604-47-7 (audio)

First Edition: December 2022

Purple Realm Publishing

War of Hearts

USA TODAY BESTSELLING AUTHOR

TAYA RUNE

Purple Realm
PUBLISHING

To receive up-to-date information, news and exclusive offers
online please sign up for the Taya Rune newsletter.

www.tayarune/subscribe.com

Taya's Steamy Books

<u>**Steamy Contemporary**</u>

Champagne Resolutions
New series coming 2023
Hollywood Themed

<u>**Steamy Fantasy**</u>

The Charming Thief

The Right To Rule Series

Outcast

Lethal

Fatal

Enchanted Underworld
Weapons of the Fae Queen Series

The Warlock's Lair

The Oracle's Court

Check out her website for all her current works.

tayarune.com

Content Warning

If you are concerned about content, please check Taya's website for a
list of warnings for all of her books.
It can be found under the **Books** tab.

tayarune.com

Without trust you have nothing.

Contents

Chapter 1

Emersyn

Emersyn turned the key to lock the front door and paused, she stared at the whitewashed wood before lifting her hand and placing it on the door. "Thank you," she whispered to the smooth surface. Thoughts gathered and Emersyn tried to push back the negative ones, the ones that had brought her back to this apartment. Instead, she attempted to focus on the positive moments. It had been a difficult year, a year spent rebuilding herself out of the broken pieces that had been left when she had discovered the truth. Now a new job offer in a new city beckoned her and nothing was holding her here.

Someone cleared their throat behind her and she smiled in spite of her heavy heart. "Are you ready, Miss Emersyn?" Harvey asked.

"I'll be there in a moment."

"I shall meet you by the car."

She waited for his footsteps to retreat before she slowly lent forward and touched her forehead to the door. Her brilliant burgundy hair fell in a straight sheet on either side of her face. A single tear escaped Emersyn's large, emerald eyes as she tried to recapture the happier times she had spent here. The apartment had been originally purchased by her father for her to live in while she attended college at Notre Dame, to study accounting. A decade later it had become her haven when her life had collapsed. For a year she had hidden there, only coming out to go to work and see the odd friend, she had no desire to run into anyone from her former life. The tears dried quickly, as if she had no more to give, and Emersyn straightened her thin black pencil skirt and tucked in her sleeveless white cotton shirt, with its gorgeous large ruffled collar that continued down the front all the way to the waist. She had completed the outfit with simple patent leather pumps and a wide black patent leather belt.

Emersyn gave the door one final pat of affection before turning and walking down the stairs to the waiting Harvey.

He stood beside the chauffeur-driven hire car, in his butler uniform, showing no signs that the mid-summer heat bothered him. His bald head glistened and there was a light sheen on his pale upper lip that she noted as she moved closer. She wondered how he was going to fare in the heat that consumed Austin, Texas rather than the short hot summers they currently experienced. Harvey was approaching fifty and he looked it, with a forehead full of heavy wrinkles and a slightly spreading midsection. He had been in her life for the past four years, electing to come with her when she had returned to the spacious apartment the year prior, rather than stay and work for her ex-husband.

"I'm ready," she announced.

Harvey opened the limousine door and stood aside. Emersyn handed him her keys to the apartment so he could give them to the real estate agent who had been hired to rent the property out. "There will be a driver at Austin who knows where he is going and will have keys for the house. I am assured that it has been aired and prepared for you."

Emersyn slid into the back seat and pressed the button for the window to go down. "I will see you in a few days, Miss Emersyn."

"Thank you, Harvey. I don't know what I would do without you." She winked at him. "Enjoy your drive down, and keep her safe."

"I will."

Emersyn was envious that Harvey was going to take several days and drive her car down to Austin, while she flew to be there to be ready for work in two days. Secretly Emersyn was a fast car junkie. Sports cars were her weakness and while she thought it crazy to spend thousands on a dress or pair of shoes, spending her money on a beautiful Corvette was absolutely reasonable.

She put the window back up and settled into the back seat as Harvey waved goodbye. Emersyn checked her bag one final time for her ticket and phone before instructing the driver that they could leave. She picked up her phone and made sure her plane was still leaving on time, before seeing what the weather would be like when she landed. Then she sent off a few emails to those friends that she wanted to remain in contact with, but had not wanted the sadness of saying goodbye to.

It didn't take long to arrive at the airport and unload her one suitcase, that she would be living out of until her remaining wardrobe arrived in the next few days. Emersyn was efficiently ushered through the first-class ticket counter and directed to the executive lounge, where she ordered her favorite fries with melted cheese, and a cosmopolitan. She was always amused at the looks she received when she ordered this combo in the fancy lounge. What was it with people who had money that they became so boring and rigid? She had no one to impress, so it didn't matter what she ate or drank or where. Emersyn had moved well past the point of ever wanting to impress anyone ever again.

The flight was called over the speaker and she made her way to the boarding gate, gaining covetous glances from some waiting in the economy line and glares from others. Emersyn took out her laptop before handing over her bags to be loaded into the overhead cabinet. Taking her seat, she admired the feel of the over-sized leather seat before switching to professional mode and returning to her research on the people she would have to deal with the most at the Chalmers and Tran Advertising Agency.

A friendly steward interrupted her studying with the offer of a glass of champagne, which she gratefully accepted and privately toasted herself. "To a new job in a new city. A perfect beginning to find new friends and focusing on extending my career." She took a sip and silently added a promise to herself. *I will steer clear of men and their pretty words which turn out to be soul-destroying lies.*

Chapter 2

Arlo

A rlo nodded his head in agreeance with the beautiful woman he sat across from. *What was her name?* he thought desperately, while she spoke of her work as a 'weather girl' on one of the local stations in Austin. *Was it Amy? No that was last week.* He smiled as she finished her story. "What are your long-term plans?" he asked.

The nameless woman began to explain that she wanted to become the entertainment correspondent on the morning show she currently worked on because her passion lay in the entertainment section of media. She loved movies and music and wanted to report on those that created them and influenced the viewing of the world. She took a small sip of her champagne, her cupid red lips perfectly pouted and Arlo lost his train of thought as he imagined where he wanted them to be later that evening.

What was her name?

The conversation was interrupted by the waiter who brought out their main meals. An entree-sized salmon salad for the weather girl, who would have to watch her weight for the remainder of her life if she chose to be on television, and a large, juicy steak with potato gratin and fennel salad for Arlo. He hoped to work off most of it tonight and any residual in the gym tomorrow morning. As they ate their meal Arlo continued to question his date. Asking her personal questions and listening attentively to her answers. Going back and asking her more questions about previous conversations when at times more information was revealed.

"You are a wonderful listener," she purred as she reached over and placed her perfectly manicured hand over his and squeezed.

"I am interested in what you have to say. You are fascinating." He flipped his hand so it was now holding hers and tightened his grip in response.

This was Arlo's superpower. He was able to talk to women, and more importantly, he had discovered the truth that all anyone wanted was to be heard. He just gave his dates the opportunity to be heard, which typically led to other more satisfying things. Women will tell you what they want if you just listen to them. They like to talk; and the majority of men don't listen, so Arlo just used this to his advantage. He had noted in his teen years that his mother always had to repeat everything and continually asked if his father was listening and that she would complain that sometimes it felt like she was talking to a wall. He discovered that if he just asked questions and kept his mouth shut women would fall into his bed because they felt they had been understood.

"Excuse me, but are you, Felicity Le Guin, from the Morning Show?" a middle-aged woman with her mobile already out and ready to take a selfie interrupted their hand-holding moment.

Thank god for middle-aged women who weren't afraid to interrupt your meal for a photo with anyone who might be famous. He thought as he offered to take a photo of the two of them after watching the woman struggle to juggle the camera and bend down for a better angle. Felicity graciously smiled and sat a little taller, which accentuated her long neck and slender shoulders. Once the woman had thanked them profusely for allowing the interruption and her eye-rolling husband had dragged her away Felicity turned back to Arlo and boldly retook his hand. "Thank you for that, some men get annoyed with people approaching me."

"I don't own you, and you are a celebrity around these parts. Some men have too big an ego," Arlo said.

"We have talked about me all night, Arlo, what do you want?"

"To be honest I don't know." He shrugged. He was always truthful with women. He loved women as people, they were wonderful and he had no desire to hurt anyone, so he was always upfront with his answers when asked this question. "I am happy being the go-to guy at Chalmers and Tran. I love my work and achieving success for my clients. I like the freedom I have at the office because I've shown my value and they trust me. Long term I don't have any plans yet." He paused and waited for the next question that every woman he took out on a first date asked.

"And what about your personal life?" Felicity didn't disappoint.

"In the short term, I don't want commitment. I like dating and I like sex, but I don't want to do that with only one woman. I like women who are strong, know who they are, and aren't afraid of their sexuality." He ran his thumb over her knuckles. "Which is why I like you. You are gorgeous and know what you want. You have a career in mind that is going to take you places and you don't need to be tied to a guy when your big break comes."

Felicity blushed prettily but stared at him, not disagreeing with his assessment. "I don't think I have ever heard anyone be so clear about not wanting a relationship."

He leaned forward and whispered in her ear, which was handily available by her up-swept hairstyle. "Would you prefer me to lie and then never call you again?" He finished by planting a soft kiss just under her earlobe.

He heard her suck in her breath. "I prefer the truth," she admitted.

"Most people do." He sat back in his chair and arched an eyebrow. "Would you care to come back to my place for dessert?"

Felicity laughed, "Isn't it usually coffee?"

"That is so boring." He moved a little closer to her and lowered his voice, "I have one piece of chocolate cake in the fridge that is a perfect size to share," he paused and grinned. "You can have it with coffee if you like?"

She smothered a laugh with her napkin. "Sounds wonderful."

Arlo indicated that they were ready for the bill and he ordered an Uber.

Half an hour later found them in his upmarket, on-trend apartment having a glass of wine, the coffee forgotten, and sharing the single slice of chocolate cake, by the light of several candles and soft music playing in the background. Felicity groaned as she swallowed the last crumbs of the cake. "Do you have any idea the last time I ate cake?"

"Too long ago would be my guess." He drank the rest of his wine in a single gulp. "I have work that needs to be finished before I get to the office tomorrow. A new head of accounting has started and I have a meeting with her."

Felicity fake shuddered. "Accounting, how dull. All those numbers seem yawn-inducing." She took the empty glass from his hand. "I know something that isn't boring." She placed the glass carefully on the coffee table before leaning in to kiss him.

<hr>

Arlo lay there, spent, and enjoying the aftermath of great sex with Felicity. She had been generous and enthusiastic and he was pleased that she had agreed to sleep with him. As usual, after half an hour of contentedness, other thoughts began to creep in. He became restless and aware that he needed a shower and to finish off the work he had mentioned earlier. He took the gentle hand that rested on his chest and kissed the palm of it before slowly rising and extricating himself from the tangle of limbs that wrapped around him. "I need a shower," he announced to the sleepy Felicity.

Without further comment, he made his way into the black and white tiled bathroom that adjoined his bedroom and turned on the shower. Briskly he washed himself and his thick, wavy, short black hair. Just as he was about to turn the shower off a fake-tanned arm slid around his waist and made to move down his torso. He quickly spun around and expertly moved out of her grasp while planting a kiss on her forehead. "I'm done, the shower is all yours. Enjoy."

Felicity pouted. "Spoilsport." She said nothing further as he left the bathroom.

Arlo dried himself and dressed in a loose-fitting t-shirt and pants. Before heading out into the kitchen to clean up the glasses and cake plate and put the kettle on. While he waited for Felicity to get out of the shower and the kettle to boil, he grabbed his laptop and the manila folder that contained ideas for clients he was overseeing with his main team.

It didn't take long for the kettle to boil and he made himself an herbal tea, anything more and he wouldn't be able to sleep later. It was after midnight, as it was, he was only going to get five hours of sleep unless he skipped the gym in the morning. He heard the shower turn off and in what he considered a short time for a woman Felicity was dressed and standing in the doorway looking a little hesitant.

"Can I call you a cab or order you a ride?" Arlo asked. "I would offer you a hot drink but I do really have work to do." He indicated the laptop and folder.

"No, thank you. I have ordered an Uber; they will be here in a few minutes." She still looked uncertain.

"I had a great night. Thank you." Arlo kissed her softly. "Can we do it again sometime?"

Felicity looked relieved. "I would like that."

"I told you I wasn't after commitment, but I also never said I was only interested in a one-night stand."

Her phone pinged, she looked at it. "My ride is here."

Arlo walked her to his door and opened it for her. "I will call you next week."

She kissed him and whispered. "Thank you for dinner. I had a wonderful night."

He watched her get safely into the car before closing and locking his door. He sat down and opened the folder, sorting through a few things as he sipped his tea. After a few attempts at starting a new speech to give to a client coming in tomorrow afternoon he closed the computer and turned off the lights, it was time to go to sleep. He would just get Mrs Beaulieu, his Personal Assistant, to reschedule the appointment for the end of the week

Chapter 3

Emersyn

Emersyn waited patiently, she adjusted her black, flared skirt and made certain her teal satin blouse was tucked in. She refrained from pressing the intercom to ask her secretary for the second time where her next appointment was. *Arlo Medina is not making a good first impression*, she thought to herself. Though, if she was really honest, she had already concluded that she had already come to some unflattering assumptions about the guru of the marketing department. He had once been the hot young go-getter at some point, but now he was handing in sub-par campaigns or passing them off to his junior staff who weren't ready for it yet. Emersyn had ascertained that the only thing saving his ass from being noticed was the work his second in charge, Jaya was doing for both of them.

Emersyn Cole had always worked in the tax accounting section of giant corporations, but was now in charge of the management accounting section of a prestigious but smaller advertising agency. Emerysn was looking forward to the new challenges and having to stretch her skill set in new ways.

The first week had gone by in a blur and Emersyn still felt disorientated with the speed that everything had happened. Harvey had only arrived two days ago, just in time to hand over the car keys for her to drive herself to work. It had been soothing to slide back into the grey trimmed leather seats and put on her favorite music as she drove the twenty minutes to work. The roads weren't packed and Emersyn had remembered that it was the height of summer and families were on holiday, either staying at home or out exploring the world. She had pushed those thoughts down, shying away from the word 'family' and concentrated on finding the right building and figuring out where to park.

"Arlo Medina has finally arrived Ms Cole," the aggrieved voice of her secretary, Charley interrupted her musings.

Emersyn couldn't help but smirk at the inflection in Charley's voice. *We are going to get along just fine,* she noted. "Send him through. Thank you, Charley."

Arlo Medina opened the door and Emersyn's immediate response was wariness. The man was gorgeous. He had beautiful olive skin and dark wavy hair, heavy eyebrows accentuated large, almond-shaped deep brown eyes. A strong nose and square jaw that was going against trend by being cleanly shaven completed the handsome face. There was obviously Mediterranean heritage with a surname of Medina and that combination of hot. She guessed he was about 5 foot 10, as she was sitting down and that he wasn't averse to spending time working out by the way his white linen shirt and dark grey trousers hung on him.

She stood and held out her hand. He grasped her hand in his and she was pleased to see that his handshake was firm but not overly so. She never understood men that felt the need to squeeze your hand so tightly or to be weak as if your hand might break.

"I'm sorry I was late. I had a client on the phone that needed attending." He apologized breezily.

She wasn't sure she believed him but knew she couldn't call him on it...yet. "Please sit," she indicated one of the plush office chairs that sat opposite her desk. Emersyn noted that he had not brought anything with him to take notes. Was he that confident of his work and place at the firm? Without preamble, she opened the folder on her desk and took out the top sheet of paper. "This is the latest account you are working on and I understand you had a meeting scheduled for this afternoon. Could you please explain the proposal to me a little more than this meager outline you have supplied and also why you postponed the meeting?"

Emersyn watched as Arlo frowned and then leaned forward to look at the paper, she had turned around for him to read. He narrowed his eyes and stared at it a little longer.

"Is there a problem?" she asked.

"I didn't bring my reading glasses?" he admitted.

"That seems rather unprepared of you. What did you think this meeting was about, Mr Medina?"

"Please call me Arlo." He smiled charmingly.

Not a chance, she thought to herself. "You didn't answer my question. What did you think I wanted to meet you for?"

"Well, I wasn't sure. George would give me a quarterly report and tell me how much money I had made the company and how pleased everyone was of me."

Emersyn was heartily sick of hearing how George handled things. It was the third time today that she had been compared to George. She was beginning to understand that George was barely more than a cheerleader for the heads of each division. He emailed them a report that gave them a basic breakdown of their financial statements every four months and a pat on the back, without any real accountability. Emersyn had been employed to break down exactly what each department was spending and earning and to make certain they were as profitable as possible as well as to make certain that the junior accountants, who were in charge of payroll, etc were doing their job efficiently. She found the job challenging and rewarding and the perfect distraction to move forward with her life.

"George was great, but he is gone. I am looking over everyone's work to see how things operate and ways in which I can help streamline processes and make the company more profitable. And this is an advertising firm and you are the head of it, which makes you the man who has to perform or everyone else doesn't get paid."

"You mean to make things cheaper?" he challenged.

"No, just more efficient," Emersyn countered. "And the reason you put off this afternoon's meeting?"

Arlo looked uncomfortable. "I have had to postpone the meeting as everything has not fallen into place as I had hoped."

"Can you tell me the broad details of this account by the end of the day?"

Emersyn watched Arlo, she tried to make up her mind how to motivate this talented man into getting him to work at full capacity again. He needed to not only step up with his clients he needed to be overseeing his juniors better and teaching them. "I would still like you to report to me a few more details than what is contained in this lackluster report by the end of today." She waved the piece of paper around.

"I have a date," Arlo announced like it was a reason to not get his work done.

"And?" She knew he was testing her to see how much of a ball breaker she was. She hated the term, it was so misogynistic, but if that's what she needed to be perceived to get the job done that she was hired to do then so be it.

"I'll let her know I may be late."

"Excellent, I look forward to seeing you at the end of business."

"Ms Cole, Mr Medina is here to see you."

Emersyn looked at her phone and was pleased to see that this time he was on time. "Send him in."

"Mr Medina, I hope your day has been fruitful," she stood as he entered the room and took the chair he had sat in earlier.

Without preamble, he launched into a more detailed account of what they had planned for the launch of the product they had been hired to do. She listened attentively, taking notes and asking the occasional question. She did note that this time Arlo had brought his reading glasses and a notepad and pen. Once he had finished explaining his team's plans, he sat waiting for her to comment.

"That's it?" She was incredulous. "It is entirely too similar to your marketing plan for the Too Yummy Beef Company launch you implemented last year. It was a great success, I'll give you that, but I'm certain that Beach Reads Publishing is not paying for the same rehash. Have you done your homework on the company and what would work well in the market, because I can't imagine radio having the same impact as perhaps Instagram with the bookstagram hashtag for this account? TikTok also seems to be gaining traction in the book marketing area."

She wondered if he had lost his creative streak? His ideas were flat and stale. Maybe he needed a holiday to recharge? Being creative all the time took a great deal of effort as far as she understood. She had always admired the creative people in her life for their ability to make something out of nothing. Emersyn looked at Arlo's smug, handsome face and changed her opinion immediately. She had a suspicion that he was lazy and happy to just get by and had simply been cruising through the past year or so. Just churning out the same old stuff and hoping his team came up with creative slogans and logos to hide the fact it was the same schtick.

Emersyn waited for him to answer. The accusation that he had just reused an idea sat there.

Arlo adjusted his grey textured tie and took off his black-rimmed glasses. "I'm impressed." He smiled innocently.

Emersyn ignored the tightness she felt in her lower stomach, the man was gorgeous, there was no denying her attraction to him, but he was also used to getting his own way with women, that was obvious. *Well, not this woman*, Emersyn thought, *I've had enough arrogant men to last me a lifetime.* She waited for him to continue.

"You have certainly done your homework," Arlo finally conceded.

"Of course, I have." She was exasperated by his nonchalant attitude. "This is an advertising company, you are the prime money maker, I am the head management accountant. It is my job to know what you are doing. Especially as your profits appear to be dropping off."

"As I said before George never had any complaints."

"Well, George is no longer here and I am. When has your meeting with Beach Reads Publishing been rescheduled to?"

"Monday, just after lunch."

"Great. It's Wednesday so I am giving you the rest of the week and weekend to get a new proposal together that I want to see with your team first thing Monday morning. Don't leave this up to your team, put the work in yourself. I also want the complete costings involved." She paused and waited for him to say something.

He sat there, a bemused look on his square features.

"Okay, well I'll see you Monday. Have a lovely date." She wanted the meeting to be over, so stood and hoped he would get the idea.

Arlo stood and gathered his glasses and notepad. "Thank you, I will."

Chapter 4

Arlo watched the elevator doors close and then began to swear loudly into the empty space. "Who does she think she is?" He had thought the meeting this morning was going to go perfectly when he walked into Emersyn's office and discovered a stunning woman sitting there. He loved women and this one was gorgeous. She had her rich burgundy hair up in a bun, her heavy bangs sat just above her round emerald eyes and her skin was flawless ivory, she must never go out in the hot summer sun to remain so fair. She wore little makeup and he noted when she held out her hand her nails were clear lacquered and short. This was a woman who knew who she was and didn't need anyone's affirmation. The meeting had ended in disaster and the second one this afternoon had been worse. Who exactly was Emersyn's boss and could he speak to them about what she was demanding of him and his staff?

He fumed as the elevator dinged and the doors slid open. "Jaya?" he called as he marched down the hallway.

His second in charge poked her head out of her office door as he arrived in the shared reception area between their offices. "Yes, boss?"

He stopped and took in Jaya and noted the empty desks of their PA's, he thought through what he wanted to say. Arlo changed his mind and asked something different, "Any word from HR on how the interviews for the new secretary are coming along?"

Jaya rolled her pale brown eyes at him. "Any chance you would consider having a male secretary for the department so we don't need to keep replacing them?"

"Just get me the most qualified." He winked at Jaya. "Though that usually means a woman. Men tend to want to work up from the mail room for some bizarre reason and don't want to go through the ranks in the same way women do."

"I wouldn't have thought it mattered to you as you frequently reassign them to different areas." Jaya countered.

"I like to help people out, secretaries are often overlooked, usually because they hire those men we were just alluding to. And I know it's a bit of a running joke in the office, but the department hasn't gone through that many secretaries."

Jaya shrugged. "Mrs Beaulieu will not be happy with you. How many times does she end up doing the secretary work for the department because she is your PA?"

"Perhaps Mitchell can help us out? Your PA is just as fabulous as mine."

"You're a flatterer, but I wouldn't let Mrs Beaulieu hear you say that," Jaya warned.

"Please?" pleaded Arlo

Jaya relented with a laugh. "Fine, I will tell Mitchell that he has to take on a few of the jobs, so we don't overwhelm your poor PA."

Arlo smiled with true gratitude. He should not sleep with the secretaries, he stayed away from them for months, it had been a year this time, but in the end, he usually succumbed to their advances. *Maybe I should consider a male secretary so the temptation is just not there, but then I could be accused of discrimination.* He was in a no-win situation. "Now, if you will excuse me, I am off to throw a tantrum in the privacy of my own office and then, while I wait for my date, get some work done for the dragon that has taken over George's job in accounts."

He stalked off into his office and closed the door. His thoughts still very much trying to figure out just how much power this new accountant had and why he had to answer to her?

The evening had gone well so far. This was their second date and Arlo had enjoyed himself. Milly was an Elementary School teacher that he had met by chance while grabbing a coffee outside his local gym. She was kind, funny and entertaining, and extremely attractive, with a deep burnished tone to her black skin and stunning hazel eyes that he found mesmerizing when she spoke passionately about her favorite students. They sat in his go-to tiny pizzeria, just two blocks from his place, on the second-floor balcony. The night sky was clear and the stars were putting on a show. Thankfully the heat from the day had abated enough that it was now pleasant rather than stifling. They had parked Milly's car out the front of his place, which Arlo took as a good sign, and had walked the few blocks to the Italian restaurant.

"You seem to be a little distracted tonight, Arlo. Is everything okay?" Milly asked in her sweet voice.

"Sorry, I had a rough day at work. The new accountant is out to prove her worth and is going over all departments and ways for us to make more money." He waved his hand, hoping to wave away his growing anger. This was not date conversation. The waiter came over and cleared the now empty pizza tray. Arlo grabbed his beer glass and drained the last of it. "How can I make my inattentiveness up to you?" He stared at her without blinking, expressing without words exactly what he had in mind.

Milly giggled, "Do you have any cake in your fridge?"

Arlo grinned. "As a matter of fact, I have two slices of New York cheesecake leftover. We could split a piece or if you are feeling indulgent you can have a piece all to yourself."

"I love cheesecake, but I don't want to get greedy, so sharing it is fine with me."

"What a sweet lady you are, Milly. Though I must warn you the nasty accountant has me jumping through hoops, so I won't be able to play all night. I have work to do."

—◆—

"That was wonderful," Arlo murmured into Milly's ear before planting a gentle kiss on her forehead. "Thank you."

They hadn't made it to the bedroom this time. A half-eaten piece of cheesecake was still on a plate on the kitchen bench and there were clothes scattered around the floor of his spacious living area. They lay entangled on the floor, having slid off the couch earlier on in the evening.

"Mmm," Milly answered without opening her eyes, but a satisfied smile appeared on her full lips. "You were fabulous."

Arlo waited for her to open her eyes, kissed her again then helped her stand and find her clothing. He didn't bother getting fully dressed, he just pulled on his trousers. He would have a shower once she left. Without appearing to hurry her he thanked her again for a great evening and promised that he would call her soon. Milly smiled and appeared to be happy with that, which matched the signals she had been giving off all night. It was rare to find a woman that wasn't always searching for more or seeking affirmation of something. In his personal life, they always tended toward the needy he had discovered.

He put the kettle on and went to have a quick shower, only wearing pj bottoms when he came out. The house was still warm and he didn't want to turn on the cooling. Arlo made himself his herbal tea and grabbed his laptop from his briefcase.

"I can't imagine radio having the same reach as perhaps Instagram for this account," he mimicked the higher-pitched voice of a woman. "What does she know about which media platforms to use for which accounts?" he muttered under his breath as he switched on the laptop and waited for it to fire up.

Now I need to prove to Emersyn how wrong she is about me. He had considered the idea of going over her head, but in the end, what could he say? That the accountant Chalmers and Tran had employed was doing their job exceedingly well and expecting the same from everyone else? That would only reflect poorly on him and perhaps George, who had been letting things slide for a while now.

Arlo absently tapped his front teeth with a pen as he looked at the proposal, he had hastily created this afternoon. "Not your best work," he admitted to himself. "No wonder she was underwhelmed." He opened a new file on his computer and typed in the title Beach Reads Publishing, just the way he used to when he was new and keen to show anyone and everyone just how good he was. Without purpose he just let his mind wander and type whatever keywords he thought of. He realized that while he had done launches for online magazine publishers before he had never worked with a true traditional publishing company that dealt with both the traditional paperback market as well as the ever-expanding eBook market and the plethora of hybrid publishers out there. It was time to do some serious research.

Chapter 5

Emersyn

It had been a long week and Emersyn was thrilled she had made it to Friday evening without strangling someone for pointing out that George didn't do things the same way she did. She stood in the almost empty lobby of her golden glass-fronted office building, fumbling through her favorite pink leather handbag for her keys and trying to keep her temper under control when she was interrupted by a cheerful, "Hello."

She looked up to discover a plump, tall Indian woman standing in front of her. Emersyn's eyes were instantly drawn to the tiny diamond stud in the perfect nose of the woman smiling at her. "Hi," she responded.

"I am Jaya Reynolds, Arlo Medina's right-hand woman." She stuck out her hand.

Emersyn extracted her hand from her overstuffed handbag and took the proffered hand. "It's great to meet you, I'm Emersyn, but I'm fairly certain you know who I am."

"Oh, everyone knows who you are. You have anyone who has been hiding behind George's good nature for too long up in arms and complaining bitterly that they may have to actually work again."

"Especially your immediate boss."

Jaya laughed loudly, "Yes, especially Arlo. Do you have plans for tonight? I thought we could go for a drink or two?"

Emersyn considered her options. Jaya appeared to be open and friendly and had not been quick to defend her boss when he was obviously in the wrong. That was always promising. Emersyn had no friends in Austin and it would be nice to go out and share in some girl talk. "Out for a few drinks sounds great. I've got my car here, so I'm happy to drive us."

"Perfect, I know a great place that has a rooftop bar, Tapas all night, and a live band on the second floor if you want to dance the night away."

"Sounds great, it's been a long week. Now, I just have to find my keys."

Jaya sipped on her drink and smiled cheerfully at Emersyn. "Relationship status?"

"Single. Very single and remaining that way for the rest of my life."

"There has got to be a story behind that statement."

Emersyn looked out over the city, enjoying the late evening breeze, and thought about anything other than her ex-husband. "Yes, there is a story, but everyone has a story, don't they?"

Jaya narrowed her eyes and pursed her lips, "Do they?"

"Yes, like what is the story behind your surname?"

"Ah, I hadn't thought of that," admitted Jaya. "Of course, you would have noticed the discrepancy."

Emersyn smiled warmly, hoping to reassure her. "There is no need for you to explain. I was just making a point."

"No, I don't mind. No one, but Arlo knows and I would like to keep it that way. When I first started applying for jobs in the advertising industry, I was getting no callback interviews, even though I had high marks from one of the best schools in the country. I noticed that the job at Chalmers and Tran, that I had applied and been rejected for, had not been filled so I changed my surname to Reynolds on my resume, it is a family name on my father's side from the times of the English occupation of India, but it is never used except as a middle name." She took a sip and signalled to the barman that she wanted another round of drinks. "Once I resubmitted my resume with the new name, I was called in two days later for an interview with Arlo and the rest is history."

"So, Arlo took the interview because you changed your name from Chatterjee to Reynolds?" Emersyn was disgusted. The man was not only lazy, egotistical, and rude he was also a racist.

"No, no, he had no idea. HR was to blame. They were only forwarding on what they thought were suitable candidates. He was only handed my resume once I had changed my name, he had never seen my original one. I came clean about my surname switch at the first interview. Arlo had the person responsible fired as soon as possible and everyone else had to be put through an education course on what was racist behavior."

"Why didn't you revert to Chatterjee once you were hired? It is on your payslips, after all."

Jaya shrugged. "I didn't think about it until all the paperwork had been completed and they had created my email address and business cards. I'm sure I could have had it all fixed, but by then the HR department had been shaken up and my point made."

The waiter brought over two more cocktails and allowed the ladies to quickly finish the dregs of their first ones. "Would you ladies like a Tapas menu?"

"Yes, please. I'm starving," answered Emersyn. "So, Arlo is not irredeemable? That was a swift and appropriate response to the situation." She was mildly impressed.

"Oh, he is amazing in many aspects."

"So, why haven't you succumbed to his touted charms?" Emersyn was genuinely interested in her answer.

"How do you know I haven't?"

"Call it a hunch."

Jaya laughed, "Oh, he is delicious, but his reputation proceeds him in the advertising game around here. I knew his reputation before I took the job and he was completely non-predatorial at my interview. He showed no sign of hiring me for any other reason than I was the most qualified. So, I took the chance and took the job when it was offered. Best thing I could have done."

Emersyn couldn't help but continue to question Jaya. *What was it about the man that makes you want to know all this stuff?* She asked herself. *You aren't questioning her about anyone else you have met in the last week.* "Well, that is great to know that he can be completely professional in the office. The records show that your department has changed secretaries on a more regular basis than anyone else."

Jaya coughed uncomfortably and took a sip of her espresso martini. "I don't know if I should tell you this, but the secretaries get reassigned once he sleeps with them. From the outside, I can see how bad that looks."

"Um, yes." Emersyn frowned and took a sip of her fancy cocktail, that she had forgotten the name of. She gave the information a chance to settle in. "It looks like he is coercing them into having sex with him to further their position in the company." She took another sip and sat there for a few moments. "Or, he is sleeping with them with no promises attached and then just shunts them off to another area because they have served their purpose and he is all about the chase, and once you are caught you are no longer worthy."

"You are wrong on both counts. I have worked with him for three years now and watched him move up the corporate ladder and he has taken me with him and I have never even contemplated sleeping with him," Jaya assured her.

"What makes you so different from the rest? You are beautiful and breathing." She winked to take the sting out of her words.

Jaya laughed. "True. I am beautiful." She flicked her long, dark braid over her shoulder and onto her back. "He thinks I am a lesbian."

"And you are not?" Emersyn was confused.

"I am bi, but when I first started work I was seeing a woman and she came to pick me up one night. Arlo saw me with her and jumped to a few conclusions after she kissed me hello. I have never bothered to let him know that I am into both guys and girls."

Emersyn lifted her fancy glass in respect. "Clever, without meaning to you gave him no reason to pursue you."

Jaya clinked her martini glass with Emersyn's upraised glass. "It would not have mattered anyway. He doesn't sleep with his staff. Ever. In the entire time, I have worked for him it has never happened."

"You know it still doesn't say anything about what is happening with his secretaries."

"I know this is odd to understand, but he doesn't pursue them, they chase him and he is always completely honest with the women he dates. I've heard him over the phone. I'm sure the company is aware of the revolving secretaries and has made sure everything is above board. If you are concerned you could always go to HR about it."

Emersyn thought about it. Was there a concern or was she looking for something because she didn't trust men and he set off every alarm she had? *You have access to everything, if there is something wrong going on you will find it,* she assured herself. "Tell me why you like working with him so much."

"He is exceptional. His ideas are current and on-trend, but he is always able to understand the market we are appealing to. He listens to the client and their needs and he is always willing to listen to team members' ideas."

"He sounds like a great boss. What I saw this week, however, doesn't reflect that, and I've done my research so I do know how exceptional he is. I am just hoping I will see something of the exceptional, not the lazy at the meeting on Monday morning."

"He will be ready," Jaya sounded confident. "We all will."

Chapter 6

Arlo

Arlo was exhausted but pleased with his efforts. It was Sunday afternoon and he was putting the final touches on his proposal for Beach Reads Publishing. He was sitting at the large dark polished oak table reviewing his spiel one final time while waiting for his hand-picked team to arrive. The conference room felt like it gave him a home ground advantage in some ways and he loved presenting there, rather than going to a client. His team were coming in to help set up and to go over everything for tomorrow's meetings, first with Emersyn and then with the client.

"Good afternoon, Arlo." Jaya smiled as she waltzed through the open door. She carried a plastic container of assorted cakes, with napkins and paper plates piled on the top of the box. Mitchell, Jaya's PA followed behind carrying a tray of three takeaway coffees. "I brought Mitchell to take notes if needed, as we don't have a secretary as yet."

Arlo ignored the bait and changed the subject. "Did you have a nice weekend while I have been working hard on this presentation?"

Jaya raised her perfectly shaped dark eyebrows at him. "You worked ALL weekend?"

"Well, I did have to eat dinner and sleep." Arlo smirked. He had managed to still meet Felicity for dinner Friday night and Sarah had been Saturday night.

"And you don't seem to be able to do those things alone," Mitchell joined in the teasing.

"Not true, I sleep alone very well."

Before anyone had anything further to add several more team members arrived. "I did do something fun this weekend," Jaya went on as she opened the box of goodies and set out a few plates and napkins.

"I had drinks with Emersyn Cole on Friday night."

Everyone stopped what they were doing and looked to Arlo. He had made it clear how he felt about the new accountant.

"Oh." Was the only response they got from him.

Jaya went on as she settled into the seat next to her boss. "You should see her car. It is freakin' awesome."

"Is she nice?" Taylah, one of the team's specialists in Social Media marketing asked.

"Yes, she was easy to talk to and fun. And so over hearing about how George did things."

They all laughed, as they had heard Arlo and a few others complaining about this over the past few days. Arlo didn't laugh, he scowled at Jaya and bit his tongue. He would not be drawn into the conversation about the woman who was making his life difficult. He hoped after tomorrow's meeting she would back off and let him get on with his work. He chose to ignore the fact that this whole thing wouldn't have happened if he hadn't of started to slack off at some point. Now he had had time to work on this project he was willing to admit, though only to himself, that he should have been doing better and he had been not only letting himself down but his team and the company.

He ignored the conversation that was happening around him, about the fancy blue sports car that Emersyn drove and made a few final adjustments to his speech before he cleared his throat and gained everyone's attention. They were still waiting on Matilda, the main events co-ordinator, she was Australian and full of energy that Arlo had always found invigorated him.

He was just about to begin when she strode in and apologized in her Aussie accent, which had taken him quite some time to understand. Australian's spoke quickly and expansively, while American's, especially those where Arlo lived, spoke slower and with just as strong an accent. Her assistant, Claire, followed more slowly as she was seven months pregnant. Everyone waited patiently while Claire settled into her seat and took out her notepad and paper.

Arlo was always astounded at how much the team still worked with pen and paper rather than on their laptops when they met. "Okay, let's get started." He pressed a few buttons on his laptop and the first slide of his presentation came up on the big screen, which took up a large section of an end wall. "As you know, usually I would have included you in the creation of this account and I am open to any feedback you have, but you are aware that my butt is on the line tomorrow morning, so I needed to prove this to myself as well as the new person in accounting." He refused to say Emersyn's name, it was petty, but he didn't care. "Let us show her exactly what type of creative team we are."

———◇———

"I am impressed." Emersyn looked around the room and smiled warmly at each team member until she got to him, Arlo noted. "I would be excited to attend a launch like this," she announced. "Now, I need a few moments alone with your boss."

Arlo noted that Jaya winked at Emersyn on the way out. He also found Matilda mouthing 'good luck' to him as she disappeared out the door.

Once they were alone, she spoke without preamble. "I will be keeping an eye on your work, as is my job. But if you produce more inspiring work like that, I see no reason why we can't get this company not only back on track but earning more money in a very short turn around."

"There is a problem here at Chalmers and Tran?" Arlo was concerned, he hadn't heard anything about it.

"Nothing to worry about. The figures are my department and yours is the creative side."

"We could make a great team," he blurted before he had even realized, he had done it. *Idiot! Now she is going to think you are interested in her. Can you not talk to a woman without flirting?*

"I'm hoping that we all make a great team." She looked him directly in the eyes, her emerald eyes flashed as she went on. "You just need to find a secretary that lasts more than six months."

He couldn't help it, he blushed and he bent his head down on the pretence of tidying up his laptop and notepad. Damn, she knew about the secretaries, he wondered what she had heard, probably nothing good. *Stupid rumor mill.*

"Good luck with meeting the client this afternoon." She gathered her things and left the conference room.

The smell of her perfume lingered and Arlo tried to ignore it as he attempted to refocus on the upcoming meeting and avoid the sinking feeling he had that she was never going to change her opinion of him now. He wondered why it mattered.

Chapter 7

Emersyn

Emersyn checked her appearance in the bathroom mirror. Her burgundy hair, which was up in a French roll, was losing its sheen, she would need to ask Jaya if she could recommend a great hairdresser. She tucked in a few stray strands and adjusted several pins. Today she wore a geometric, black and white patterned, form-fitting mid-thigh length dress, that had no sleeves and an asymmetrical neckline. The pattern on the dress was bold, so she had chosen to wear minimal jewelry in silver tones. Emersyn applied a layer of tinted lip gloss and then frowned at herself. *You are going out to lunch with Jaya, why all the preening?* She asked herself. She chose not to consider the answer as she checked her phone for the time and realized that she was now late and hurried from the bathroom.

Jaya was standing with a petite, natural red-headed woman with a cute pixie cut, who Emersyn guessed was in her mid-twenties. Emersyn hung back, not wanting to interrupt, but Jaya signaled her over. "Come and meet the new department secretary, Eva."

Eva smiled to reveal a perfect row of small white teeth and stuck out her slender, small hand. "Hi, lovely to meet you."

Emersyn shook her hand. "Hi, welcome to the Agency. I'm Emersyn, I work in accounts."

"She is being modest," Jaya interrupted. "Emersyn is the head management accountant at the firm. She keeps us all on our toes. Especially, Arlo." She winked.

Eva looked a little less sure of herself and Emersyn felt bad. "I'm not that scary. It will be wonderful to have someone here that can answer my emails without bothering the different sections of the marketing team, as you will be compiling the monthly reports. I will schedule a meeting with you for early next week, once you have had the chance to settle and meet everyone, to discuss what I will need from you each month."

"Sure, there a lot of people to meet. I am looking forward to working here, but I had no idea how many different sections of advertising there were." Eva looked a little flustered.

"You'll be great. They wouldn't have hired you if they didn't think you were capable and don't forget that several of them have PA's, so you won't need to worry too much about that work," Jaya reassured her.

As Jaya and Eva chatted Emersyn considered whether to warn her about Arlo. She seemed lovely and innocent, with her pretty white summer dress, that had little forget-me-nots on it, and her strappy mid-heeled sandals. *She's not eighteen, I'm certain that she is not as naive as I was. Jaya reassures me that I have misunderstood Arlo so maybe I should just mind my own business and keep an eye on things instead.*

"I'm starving, are you ready for lunch?" asked Jaya as Eva waved goodbye and headed back to her desk.

"Absolutely. Where are we going today?" Emersyn had been guided by Jaya's extensive knowledge of where to eat near their office building over the last few weeks and hadn't been steered wrong yet.

"How do you feel about Japanese?"

"Love it."

As they went to leave, they were interrupted by a male voice calling Emersyn's name.

———◆———

Arlo

Arlo watched through his reception office door as Emersyn and Jaya walked by, off to lunch he assumed. Just as they moved out of his line of sight, he heard Emersyn's name being called. Curiosity got the better of him and he stepped out into the corridor to see who was calling her. Arlo was surprised to see Henry Tran, one half of Chalmers and Tran Advertising Agency rushing down the deep blue carpeted corridor. Henry Tran ran the Texas office, while Gibson Chalmers ran the New York office.

"Ah, Arlo. Just the person I was looking for."

"I thought you were calling Ms Cole, Mr Tran?" Arlo tried not to show his confusion.

"Yes, yes. I was calling both of you. I was on my way down to see you, Arlo then was heading up to accounts to find Emersyn. It is most fortuitous that you are both here. Can I have a word with both of you in Arlo's office, please?" Mr Tran was impeccably dressed in a navy pinstriped three-piece Armani suit; which Arlo thought was an insane choice for the middle of the oppressive summer that was typical of Austen. He was short, confident, and quietly spoken with the slightest trace of a Vietnamese accent.

Arlo noted that Emersyn looked uncomfortable as she quietly spoke to Jaya and moved toward his office. He stood aside to let her through the door and noted again how wonderful she smelled. He had reported to her every Monday morning for the past three weeks about his team's ideas, and progress. But that was the only time he saw her and they never spoke of anything other than the newest idea or client. He knew she was settling in fine to the city and that Jaya now spent every Friday night with her, partying to the wee hours. *Maybe Emersyn isn't giving you anything because she is a lesbian, you idiot? She is hanging out with Jaya all the time now.*

Mr Tran indicated for Arlo to take a seat on the richly upholstered beige lounge, that took up a large part of his huge, stunning corner office. Arlo chose the corner seat, closest to the window on the low, wide three-seater couch. Emersyn chose one of the two single seats and Henry Tran took the opposite seat to Arlo on the three-seater couch.

Without any warning, he launched into what he had come down to tell Arlo. "I want both of you to go to LA on Monday to meet with a potential client. This a wonderful opportunity for us to explore the LA market and extend our exposure. They have requested you personally, Arlo. They've heard that you are on top of your game and that they would prefer to deal with us than the New York office," he sounded like a proud father. He turned to Emersyn. "I'm sending you along to make sure the numbers work. I am impressed with the way you have improved costs already and are picking up the advertising game, this will give you a chance to see a different side of it. You will be able to see how we start from the ground up and hopefully, you might be able to streamline a few things."

"I'm flattered that you think I would be beneficial to the venture," Emersyn enthused. "I look forward to working side by side with Mr Medina and learning all I can."

Arlo was surprised that she could sound so sincere, yet her eyes lacked any real emotion. He was at a loss to understand how she truly felt and if he was honest, he didn't know how to feel about spending time with her. "How long do you think we will be away? And who is the company we are meeting?"

He watched Emersyn flush, as she was probably kicking herself for not asking those exact questions.

Mr Tran answered, "I want you prepped before you go. Monday you will fly out and that afternoon meet with them to ascertain their wants - they are being tight-lipped about the details. Work together for two days and present your basic ideas to them on Thursday and fly home Friday." He got up to leave, "Oh and the client is Happy Girl Enterprises."

Arlo fought for control of his jaw as his stomach fluttered with nerves and his jaw wanted to drop in shock. Happy Girl Enterprises was a big deal. "This is highly unusual to do it this way," commented Arlo. "We typically have some idea of what we are walking into and more time to prepare even a basic presentation."

"Oh, I know, but that is their request and they would be quite the coupe if we could get their account. So, we play by their rules." Henry Tran looked at both of them for several moments. "You are both capable. Do what you do best and get this done."

Chapter 8

Arlo

Arlo was getting out of his cab when a blue corvette pulled up behind them. He watched with dawning recognition as a man, around fifty in a crisp butler uniform got out of the passenger side and came around to open the door on the magnificent car and helped the driver, Emersyn, out. He then moved to the boot and took out a large suitcase, that had a matching carry-on bag, hanging garment bag, and beauty case. Arlo finished collecting his own garment bag and suitcase from the cab and moved slightly away from the sports car and the attention it was drawing. He continued to watch with fascination as Emersyn waited patiently by the car and her luggage while the butler went to get a luggage trolley for her. A few people asked her questions about the car, which she appeared to answer enthusiastically. Eventually, a trolley was found and the matching luggage stacked. Emersyn gave the butler the keys and a warm hug before she turned to push the trolley through the closest doors.

He didn't know why, but Arlo chose to hang back, rather than call out to her as she moved past him. She made him nervous for some reason. All his usual charm didn't appear to work on her. Emersyn had told him over the last month that the work his teams were putting out was incredible and business was steadily growing again as word spread that Arlo was on his game. It was a great confidence boost but all her flattery derived from work. He counted to twenty before walking through the departure doors and heading to the airline counter, only to discover Emersyn standing in the queue. He hadn't considered that because they were flying Business Class that there wouldn't be too many people queuing up.

"Hi, how are you?" Emersyn asked as he approached.

"Great, and you?" he asked as they moved up to the front of the line.

"I am looking forward to seeing how this all works from the beginning."

The impeccably dressed lady at the check-in counter beckoned Emersyn over. "I'll see you later."

Arlo smiled. "Sure." He watched her walk over to the counter, admiring her bare calves in her patent leather black high heels and knee-length white pencil dress. *She is your work colleague; she is a lesbian and you will look like a creep if you get caught staring at her.* He busied himself with making sure he had his ID and ticket ready.

A cough behind him alerted him to the fact that he was being called to the counter. He looked up to find Emersyn nowhere in sight. After checking in, he browsed the shops and bought lollies to suck on when they were taking off so his ears didn't hurt. He sat for a while watching an older couple chatting at a cafe, sipping coffee and holding hands across the table. It felt odd to witness it as his parents had never shown much affection. Before long, his flight was being announced that they were ready for boarding.

Only as he was ushered onto the plane and directed to his seat did he think of the seat that would be filled next to him. There was a partition between them but it was not as high as on many other planes and it would be quite easy to chat over. He would have to sit next to Emersyn for over three hours. The thought of sitting next to a beautiful woman for so long would usually have made him happy, but today it just filled him with dread. He had no clue as to why she had this effect on him, but he didn't enjoy the feeling. As he waited for Emersyn to arrive, he decided to at least look like he was working and completely relaxed, so pulled out his laptop before stowing his carry bag away. While he waited for the flight attendant to offer him a drink, he pulled up the research he had been doing on Happy Girl Enterprises.

"Hello, again," Emersyn spoke brightly as she moved to the seat next to his. A flight attendant waited patiently, holding Emrsyn's garment bag while she took out her laptop and organized a few things before handing the attentive flight attendant her carry-on luggage. "Can I please have a Chai Spiced Tea?" She paused and looked over at Arlo. "Have you ordered anything yet?"

"Mimosa, please."

The flight attendant nodded. "Of course, but you will have to wait until we have completed take off before I can serve any hot beverages. I'll get you your Mimosa, Sir."

"Thank you," they both answered.

Arlo went back to his reading, trying his best to ignore the growing temptation to talk to her. It was a battle he lost. "I have been reading up on Happy Girl Enterprises and their rise through the ranks of cosmetic companies has been phenomenal. All on the back of stick-on nail polish."

Emersyn appeared interested. "Yes, from original launch to global domination in the teen market in five years is something to be studied and learned from."

Arlo was impressed, she had been doing her homework. "What is your take on it?"

"I think what they do that is different to everyone else is they aren't selling the dream they are selling the reality. Their market is teen girls and teen girls are savvier than ever before, they know if they buy lipstick from an endorsed celebrity and use it, they won't end up looking like the celebrity. What they are selling is self-confidence. You can wear their nail stickers and feel happy and pretty just as you are. The nail stickers were brilliant because they can be applied and removed with minimal fuss. So, if you go to a school with strict uniform codes or a job where you aren't allowed to wear polish you can be ready to go out in five minutes rather than the half an hour it takes to apply and wait for it to dry, no matter how many products other companies sell that claim that they can dry nails in a few minutes."

"That was a very clear take on exactly what they did and what they built on. No wonder Henry hired you."

Emersyn smiled. "If you are going to be a company CPA rather than one for families and small businesses you need to be willing to understand the business you work for or you will stay at the bottom of the rung, processing the stationary data forever."

"Where did you start your journey of processing stationery?" Arlo laughed.

"Toyota."

"So, you are from Chicago?"

"No, it's near where I went to school and straight out of there to Toyota."

Arlo found himself on steady ground, he was back in his element. Asking a woman questions, though he did note that she hadn't given any more information than she needed to. "Where did you go to college?"

"Notre Dame, Mendoza College of Business. My CPA exam was taken in Master of Business Administration." She rattled it off like she got the question frequently.

"One of the best in the country." Arlo was drawn to her and grateful that there was a partition between them to stop him from doing anything dumb, like trying to lean closer. Emersyn was fascinating.

When she had spoken about the client she had been enthused and animated and brilliant, now speaking about herself she was succinct and reticent.

"Where did you study?"

He was surprised that she had continued the conversation. Though, it was always polite to ask once you had been asked. "The University of Texas, Bachelor of Marketing and Communication."

"So, we are both overachievers," she chuckled.

Any further conversation was interrupted by the flight attendant returning with Arlo's Mimosa and asking them to prepare for take-off.

Emersyn

Emersyn sipped her excellent chai tea and nibbled on the delicious croissant. Oh, how she loved flying Business Class. As she did her best to try to concentrate on the screen in front of her, she was uncomfortably aware of the man seated beside her. The flight attendant came out with his requested toasted sandwich and another Mimosa and as Arlo cleaned up his area to make room for the food, he went to stow several things in the overhead compartment when a single sheet of paper floated down to Emersyn's lap. "Arlo Luis Gabriel Medina," she announced. It turned out the piece of paper was his boarding pass.

He had looked up when she had spoken his name. She held out the boarding pass for him, "That is quite a name you have there. Impressive."

Arlo grimaced and she found it secretly charming. "My mother wanted a grand name for her Spanish baby boy."

"It is grand," Emersyn agreed. "Does your mother have a grand name too?"

Arlo laughed, "No, her name is Tracy. She comes from Oklahoma and broke her parent's hearts by not going to college and taking a year to explore Europe and visit an exchange student they had had from France. She came back three years later with my Dad, who is a Spaniard, in tow. They were already married and she had only discovered that she was pregnant with my sister a week prior."

"Does your sister have a fancy Spanish name too?"

"Oh yes, she didn't escape my mother's obsession with all things Spanish. Santana Carmen Isabel Medina." He pronounced the name with a strong Spanish accent.

"That is so beautiful. Do you speak Spanish?"

"Yes, Mom learned Spanish when she was with Dad in Spain and wanted us to learn it too. We all had to speak Spanish at the dinner table every night growing up and even now if it is the four of us, she likes us to keep practicing."

"Your mother sounds wonderful." Emersyn fought to keep the wistfulness from her voice. Arlo's upbringing was very different from her own.

"She is, but she is also over the top with her insistence that we know our background on our father's side. It's like she has completely forgotten that we have two cultures to understand."

"But you live the other culture. You have been submersed in it since birth. What could she tell you that you don't already know? You sell it for goodness sake."

"Well, when you put it like that." His deep brown eyes looked sheepish.

Emersyn couldn't help it, she let out a throaty laugh. Not a polite chuckle or a cute giggle, but a proper chortle. She decided to save his ego, she didn't know why, but it mattered to her. "Or were you talking about personal history? Where her side of the family originates from? As they are just as important."

He leaped onto the notion. "Yes, that is exactly what I meant to say. It's like she is embarrassed by her Mid-Western roots."

"Have you ever asked her about it?"

The sheepish look was back. "Uh, no."

Emersyn just looked at him like he was a simpleton. "Perhaps, you should?"

Arlo laughed ruefully, "Maybe I will, when the opportunity next comes up."

"Sounds like a plan."

"What's your mom like?"

She knew the question was coming at some point and it didn't matter how many years had passed the answer always brought sadness. "My Mom died when I was eight from kidney failure. I don't have many memories of her, but the ones I do are wonderful. I always remember picnics. No matter where we lived, we had picnics."

"I am sorry about your mom. That is something you never move on from." Arlo spoke gently.

Emersyn grimaced. "Time softens everything, but you carry those things forward always."

"If it wasn't deemed as inappropriate, I would attempt to take your hand right now." Arlo smiled kindly.

Her heart lurched and she struggled to harden it again. *The man is a womanizer, you will do well to remember that this week,* she chastised herself.

"What about you? Do you want to be a mother?" Arlo asked.

Emersyn thought about it before she answered. She didn't want to reveal too much of herself, but he had been sincere in his attempts to make her feel better. "I don't know anymore," she paused and looked up at the bulkhead. "Before I got married, I would not have hesitated to say yes, but after the disaster of my marriage, I just don't know. I've seen friends and their partners use their children as pawns to avenge slights perceived after the divorce. They can tie you to an asshole forever in ways nothing else can. And my ex-husband is the biggest asshole of all." She almost spat out the last few words with venom dripping from her mouth because of the humiliation and painful thoughts the man always brought up.

Arlo raised his heavy eyebrows and then frowned, but refrained from defending the male gender at that moment. "Well, that is perfectly understandable that you would feel that way," he said cautiously.

"What about you? Do you see children in your future?" Emersyn chose not to announce the unkind thoughts that were swirling in her head. *With the number of women, I can guess you have slept with there are probably a few children you aren't even aware of yet.*

"Children are wonderful, but I'm not sure I'm the guy to raise them. I'm a great Uncle, I even know my nieces and nephews' birthdays, and never fail to show up at their big events if I can help it. BUT that is very different from being there always. I just think I might be too self-centered to be as awesome as my Dad is."

"Wow, that is honesty that you don't see too often." Emersyn was surprised by Arlo's appraisal of himself. Most people were never that open about their shortcomings.

Arlo leaned as close to the partition as possible without going over it. He spoke quietly so Emersyn had to lean in to hear him over the noise of people chatting, plane engines, and flight attendant trolleys. "I am many things, some great, some terrible, but the one thing I pride myself on is my honesty." Their heads were almost touching. "You can always trust me to be honest, even if you don't like what I have to say."

Emersyn closed her eyes and secretly breathed in the scent of the man that made her groin tighten before she spoke softly, "Trust is earnt, but I appreciate your honesty."

They were interrupted by the flight attendant who had come to retrieve the empty plates and glasses. "Another Mimosa, sir?"

They moved apart. "No, thank you. Black coffee please and another toasted sandwich if possible?"

"Certainly, sir."

Emersyn was happy to hear that he was switching to coffee. She loved a drink, as evidenced on a Friday night when she went out with Jaya, but not on a flight when they were headed to a meeting with a potentially game-changing client. She had refrained from saying anything about his beverage choice because she wasn't his mother nor supervisor but probably would have spoken up if he had had ordered a third Mimosa.

"Can I get you anything, Ma'am?" inquired the solicitous flight attendant.

"Sparkling water would be great, thank you." Emersyn settled back further into her leather seat and closed her eyes. She didn't want to talk anymore. She had told him enough.

Chapter 9

Emersyn

Happy Girl Enterprises offices were well appointed without being ostentatious. Emersyn and Arlo were ushered into a spacious conference room and offered beverages by a young male intern with a full face of make-up. Emersyn asked for a bottle of water and watched Arlo to see his reaction to the young man.

"Water would be great too, thanks." He smiled openly at the intern. "That color lipstick looks great on you," Arlo complimented him.

Emersyn was surprised, many men from Texas would not have been comfortable with the make-up wearing intern. Arlo didn't appear anything but curious.

The young man beamed. "It's from the just launched Fall Collection."

"Thank you, Sebastian, that will be all." A middle-aged man in a dark suit, with grey sprinkled through his thinning hair, walked in, followed by an entourage of people. He towered over both Emersyn and Arlo as he shook their hands. "I am Michael Bowen, CEO, and co-founder of Happy Girl."

"Pleased to meet you. Will your daughter be joining us?" Arlo inquired.

"Not today. Tiffany has a few things to take care of before she begins her final year of college. She is hoping to join us on Thursday to see what you come up with."

Sebastian came in with two bottles of water, several glasses, and a latte. He placed them on a table at the side of the room and efficiently dispensed the drinks before leaving. "Please sit and let me introduce the rest of the team."

About eight people were sitting at the table and one very attractive, but slightly artificial young lady, had a small box sitting in front of her. Michael quickly introduced everyone, but Emersyn wasn't quick enough to take it all in and also their job roles. What she did remember was the name of the box holding blonde who smiled at Arlo in a way that made Emersyn's skin crawl. Pascal was the name of the sculptured in-house marketing manager. She barely raised a smile for Emersyn but the alluring look she gave Arlo was clear. He seemed to enjoy the attention, which irked Emersyn for some reason. *Keep focused,* she chided herself.

"Pascal, please show them what we are hoping to develop a marketing campaign for." Michael went on, oblivious to the subtle flirting happening in front of him. "We started in nail care, then moved into make-up, body creams, and the obligatory fragrance range. All for teen girls, with the aim that they can be the best version of themselves and not someone they follow online. It has always had to be affordable to their part-time job budget if they aren't lucky enough to have a parent buy it for them. And also, cheap enough that a parent won't mind buying it for them, but it will feel like a treat." He paused and waited for Pascal to take the items out of the box and line them up in front of Arlo and Emersyn.

Emersyn noted that Pascal had chosen to move around her to stand beside Arlo.

Michael continued. "We present the Happy Girl Enterprises Hair Care Line."

The products lined up before them were wonderful. Shampoos, conditioners, tubs of hair masks, detangling serum, repair serum, all color-coded to match what type of hair you had.

"There is no brush here." Arlo frowned at the product range. "You are not including a brush in the launch?"

Emersyn was surprised, she had not even thought of a brush until Arlo had brought it up. As she looked around the table, it appeared she wasn't the only one.

"And that is exactly why I asked you to fly out," exclaimed Michael.

Pascal looked a little annoyed. "The brush has been a sticking point."

Arlo looked at Michael. "Is there a brush in development?"

"There are several brushes in development because one brush will not suit everyone."

"Maybe a brush for each hair type? Or a comb to go with the detangling serum?"

Pascal answered, "You don't think all those different brushes and a comb shouldn't come under hair accessories?"

"Definitely and I am assuming that is being developed as we speak and will be the next launch. But until that happens, I think it is necessary for the launch to have a complete hair care line and that includes a brush or two. Maybe two brushes that can be used for several things?"

Pascal began to answer, "I'm just not..."

Michael spoke over the top of Pascal. "Yes, Tiffany was thinking two brushes to compliment the launch range. More will be added if this launch is successful."

"Makes sense to me," Arlo agreed.

"Do you have any questions or will we just hand you the box and the information of what Pascal has already been working and you can take it and start?"

Arlo looked seriously at Michael. "I do have one question."

"Go on."

"Why me?"

Emersyn noted that he didn't ask 'why us?' or 'why Chalmers and Tran?'

Michael leaned forward in his seat, while the rest of his team sat back. "Tiffany and I thought you would suit what we need. Your work for the Better You Supplement Range two years ago was brilliant and caught our attention. The haircare market is huge, but not in the area we want to challenge in. Our goal is to knock Revlon off its perch. We did our research on you. You have a female-dominated team, which we think will be a large asset to the creating of the campaign. It also shows you are happy to listen to women, this was especially important to Tiffany, because as a young woman she is not always taken seriously. Regardless of what she has already achieved." Michael said the last sentence with great pride in his voice.

"Who would you prefer us to contact if we have questions regarding the products and budget?" Arlo asked as he started to put the bottles and tubs back into the box.

Emersyn sat up as this information pertained to why she was here. "As Tiffany is only unavailable today, she will be back on board to-morrow so until she heads to College again it's best to deal with her. After all, this is her baby. Pascal and the team run things in marketing once everything is set up, but Tiffany usually does the heavy lifting with the advertising firm with the original launch." Michael nodded at Emersyn. "I will get some figures emailed to you pronto, so you can get started immediately."

"Thank you." They were the only words she had spoken in the meeting. It felt odd to sit and not be able to contribute but that was

not her role here. Emersyn was just relieved to learn that she wouldn't
have to be dealing with Pascal while they were he

Chapter 10

Emersyn

Emersyn was grateful to fall onto the king-sized bed in her beautiful hotel room. She was still in the clothes she had travelled and attended the meeting in. She kicked off her high heels, not caring where they fell, and sighed heavily. It had been a draining day and yet she was full of enthusiasm to start the next morning immediately. She checked her phone messages and quickly shot off a text to Harvey.

H: Hey, got here safe and had the first meeting. Did everyone arrive okay?

E: Hello, yes, everyone has arrived and settled in. They were all disappointed to find you not here but look forward to spending the weekend with you.

H: Me too! Have fun with your family. E

E: Good luck with the proposal. H

Emersyn always loved the way that even in text form Harvey was still formal. She hoped he did have fun with his family. They had arranged a month prior for all of them to take holidays and to come and stay with their father and Emersyn. She had insisted that they stay at the house, as there were certainly enough rooms and it would be wonderful to have company. Unfortunately, now she would miss most of the visit due to the trip.

Dragging herself up off the bed, she went to her laptop and turned it on, carrying it back to the bed before realizing that she needed to charge it. She then wasted several minutes unpacking her suitcase, finding her charger, and finding a power point near the bedside table so she could charge it near her.

While Emersyn was standing, she decided to run a bath. As she waited for the bath to fill, she quickly jotted down a few thoughts she wanted to discuss with Arlo the next morning and then sent off a text to a friend that she was in town and were they available for a drink or two in the hotel bar tonight? Emersyn was tired but didn't want to spend the whole night in her hotel room by herself. She had spent many nights by herself over the past year if you didn't include Harvey, and she once was a very social person, and now that Jaya had reminded her of how much fun it was to be around people, she found she wanted to spend less time alone.

As she climbed into her steaming, sudsy filled tub her phone dinged.

J: Hey you! Can't believe you are in town and only telling me now. Yes, I'm free. I'll be there in two hours, just gotta wrap up a few things on this house sale. ;-)

E: Fabulous!! See you at the bar. :-)

Emersyn put the phone down, undid the French roll, she typically wore at work, and slid deeper into the bath. Exhaling with a big whoosh she put her head under the water and let herself float in the huge tub. Her mind wandered and she processed the day as she always did. The plane trip was enlightening in many ways, but also uncomfortable as she didn't like to admit that between the conversation on the plane and seeing Arlo take control in the meeting this afternoon her opinion of him was slowly changing. He perhaps wasn't as bad as she had first thought and her prejudices against men probably influenced her. His warm brown eyes and strong tanned face floated in front of her closed eyes and her body tingled. She came up for air and grabbed the soap, luxuriating in its fresh scent.

After her bath Emersyn then jumped in the shower and gave her hair a quick wash. For some reason even though she loved the bath, she never felt clean until she had a shower. The bath always left a residue on her. She hummed to herself in the shower and watched the steam form on the glass shower panels. Like a sixteen-year-old, she traced a love heart in the steam then put her initials E.C in the heart with a & underneath but instead of putting the name of her one true love she put a ?. She laughed, rolled her eyes at her childishness, and swiped her hand across it all to erase her moment of silliness. *You don't need to love anyone, just yourself. Now get your butt into gear or you are going to be late.*

"I'll have a French Martini, please," Emersyn ordered as she took a seat at the hotel's chic, blue and gold bar. The bar room was half full and people chatted cheerfully, while all the time checking out the next person that walked through the doors. This is LA, Emersyn reminded herself. Land of famous people and those that wanted to be famous. Everyone was always looking for an angle and very few people were happy with the life they already had.

"Emmy?"

Emersyn turned around and grinned as Jeremy pushed through the little groups gathered in his way. Most people stared at him as he went by, trying to recall where they had seen his face. Was he famous enough to bother? Jeremy was a tall, gorgeous black man who she had met at college and had briefly considered having a relationship with but she had put him in the friend zone when she had discovered just how much work she had to do to be at the top of her class. The reason so many people thought they recognized him was that his face was plastered on strategic billboards throughout LA advertising his real estate company. He was handsome and dressed with a 'look at me' style that they assumed was because he was an actor or musician.

"Jeremy, it is so good to see you." Emersyn stood on her tiptoes to reach his cheek to kiss him. He engulfed her in a hug that made her feel safe and loved. She hadn't felt that in a long time. It was bliss.

"You look incredible. I love the hair." He settled into the seat beside her and ordered a drink as the bartender handed over Emersyn's. "Why didn't you tell me you were coming, I could have organized to take some time off and we could have hung out, like old times."

"I'm here for work and wasn't sure if I would have any time to socialize. Sorry, it was such short notice." She took a sip of her cocktail, it was delicious. "How are things with you? Catch me up on everything."

They spent the next half hour talking about the strange, wonderful, and demanding clients that Jeremy dealt with daily. He was a realtor for mansions of the rich and famous and the encounters he had had were fascinating to listen to. "Your Dad was in town a few months back. Told me to rent out the house for another year."

"Figures, I don't think he's interested in living here any time soon, he is living with some young 'lady' in the Bahamas at the moment. And I don't need it, I am settling in nicely to Austin and the new job."

"Didn't you live in Austin when you were much younger?"

"Yes, I think we were there for about a year, just before I started schooling. They had heard that some doctor was doing great things for people with Mum's condition so Dad bought a house and moved us there. The doctor couldn't help Mum so they found another one that was full of promises and we moved here for a couple of years and I started school. Everywhere we lived Dad bought a house and we never sold the previous one, he just rented them out. Looking back, it was a clever way to pay off the properties."

"And he still owns all the houses he bought?"

"No, he owns all the houses he and Mum lived in. I think there are eight in total. As you know he gave me the apartment as a gift when I was accepted into Notre Dame."

"I was sorry to hear about your divorce. Did you have to sell the apartment as part of the divorce to Nicolai?"

Emersyn grimaced. She hated hearing his name and refused to speak it. "I kept my car and apartment and he kept everything else. I just wanted out and he was grateful because I didn't want to take him for his money."

"Oh, that is too funny. So, he still hasn't figured out that you are much wealthier than he is?" Jeremy's smile was wicked.

"I am not wealthier than he is. On paper, he has more than me. My father is wealthy and I am just lucky enough to live in stunning houses where I don't pay for anything. I pay for my cars and all my clothing and food and anything else I want," she defended herself.

Jeremy put his hands up in supplication. "Whoa, you know I don't care how much money you do or don't have. I was just letting you know that your dad was in town."

"How did he look?"

"Not great. I saw him at 10:00 am and he already smelt of alcohol."

Emersyn was not surprised. When her mother had died, her father had taken up drinking and she had been shipped off to alternating grandparents for a year or two until he said he was ready to parent again. It had been a disaster, but Emersyn had simply endured and spent as little time at home as possible. She had been grateful when her acceptance letter for Notre Dame had come. They had been living in New York at the time, the last place her mother had been alive and it had been on her bucket list to live in New York. Emersyn had never been back and she knew the Penthouse apartment mostly stood empty, only being rented out on short-term leases. The view over Central Park was spectacular and being appreciated by no one the majority of the time.

"Are you seeing anyone?" Emersyn asked, wanting to change the subject. She spoke to her father once a month to make sure he was alive, but they didn't have a relationship in any true sense of the word.

"You know me, I can't keep a girlfriend to save myself." Jeremy smiled and shrugged his shoulders. "It may have something to do with the fact that I'm never home."

They spent the next two hours reminiscing about their college days. Emersyn hadn't laughed so long in forever and it felt good to be with someone she didn't need to be guarded around. Jeremy knew her family situation and had been at her wedding. He didn't pry about what had ended her marriage, but at least she didn't have to avoid explaining anything.

As Emersyn prepared for bed, she lay out her gym clothes, just like at home, well at home Harvey did it, so when she wakes up it's the first thing she sees and gets dressed into. Pushing her to do a dreaded workout. She was one of those people who truly didn't enjoy working out in any way. Emeryn had never found an activity that made her sweat and was good for her that she enjoyed, but Emersyn knew the benefits of it for her body as well her mental health so she did it even though she hated it. Half an hour six days a week and keeping an eye on how much sugar she put in her mouth kept her fitting into her favorite clothes.

Quickly she settled into bed and fluffed up her pillow, turning on the TV to see if there were any decent Hallmark murder mysteries movies to watch. In the end, it didn't matter as she fought to keep her eyes open and she gave in and went to sleep dreaming of brown eyes that turned to ice blue and feelings of betrayal.

Chapter 11

Arlo

Tap, tap, tap. The pen hit Arlo's teeth as he walked slowly around the conference table. He struggled to remain on topic as what he wanted to know was who Emersyn had been having drinks with the night before. He had spotted them at the bar as he came down to confirm everything that was needed for the use of the conference room. At first, he had not recognized her as her hair had been down and she only ever wore it up at work. She had been laughing and looked relaxed, sipping on her drink and casually reaching out and touching the person she spoke to.

They had been in the conference room for almost two hours. Emersyn had been emailed the budget Happy Girl was willing to spend on their campaign and Arlo had read through all of the product information they had provided. He was struggling to put himself in the shoes of a teenage girl. As a teenage boy, girls had been a mystery to him and so it had stayed until he realized if he listened to them and was honest, they would be willing to be with him. He now wished he had taken more notice of his sister's teen years, but she had always kept him away from her private life as he was just her annoying younger brother.

"Is this the way you usually work?" Emersyn interrupted his musings.

"No. It's not. Usually, I've come up with and discarded several ideas by now," he was honest with her. "I'm struggling to get a handle on the right path for this. By the look of it, the budget is big enough to do this any way we want and that might be hindering me."

"Okay. What else is bothering you?" She pushed him.

He laughed. "Is that not enough?"

"I am sure you have had times where you get to spend whatever you want. To me, that doesn't appear to be much of a reason." Her emerald eyes stared at him. "You told me you were always honest," she accused.

Arlo groaned. "Fine, but it is kind of embarrassing." He pulled out a chair and sat down. He sat on the opposite side of the table to Emersyn. "Every time I think of shampoo and ideas I end up with naked women in showers, that is totally age inappropriate and creepy."

Emersyn looked like she was trying to keep a straight face.

"It's okay, you can laugh."

Without a word, Emersyn began to laugh, a delightful throaty laugh that made Arlo join in. "I suppose that when we think of ad campaigns for hair care we get sexy women in showers," she agreed.

She had a flashback to the night before and her shower. "I may have a suggestion if you are willing to listen?"

"I'm always open to new ideas. Suggest away."

"Well teenage girls in showers sing and draw love hearts with initials in them on the shower screens as it gets foggy. They sing into their hairbrushes as well."

"They do?" Arlo was astounded. "And you did this?"

"Well, a long time ago, but yes." She omitted last night's lapse into teenage hood.

"That is wonderful and funny and kinda silly."

Emersyn quickly grew defensive. "Well, what were you doing in the shower as a teenager?" She stopped and grinned. "On second thought, don't answer that."

Arlo had the grace to blush.

They were interrupted by his laptop beeping. Jaya was requesting a Facetime call. He hit the button and her friendly face filled the screen, her diamond nose stud glinted as she turned. "Hey guys, how are you both this morning?"

"I think Emersyn has just come up with the basis of our campaign." He quickly went on to describe what she had just revealed to him.

Jaya gasped, "That is perfect. I did that too. Though I had to sing a bit quieter as Mum always complained about the terrible American music I was listening to." She winked through the screen at Emersyn. "That has some real potential. I'll start the team working on slogans and creating content mock-ups for the social media blitz and leave you two with the main ad copy. I'll be in touch with both of you once I have some basic costings and ideas."

Arlo had been only half paying attention to Jaya. "Okay, I'll talk to you later." His mind had leaped onto Emersyn's idea and was thinking up some new twists on it. "What about instead of them putting someone's initials in the love heart on the shower screen they put the bottle of shampoo and conditioner? And they can be in cute pajamas, rather than sexy towels, in the bathroom detangling their hair and singing into their Happy Girl hairbrush?" He was talking out loud while jotting down ideas. "We need to know what teenage girls are into watching and listening to at the moment. What TV shows and what time slots and networks as well as any movies that have a release date in theaters around the launch date."

"I can start that for you. I can't do costings until we have firmer plans and I think this is why Henry sent me with you." Emersyn looked eager to start.

"Why do you think he sent you?"

"To truly understand what it is you all do and to see how this grows from idea to final product and how long it takes." She shrugged. "To see why it costs us so much."

Arlo was smart enough to not say anything about answering to her and her never-ending questions about how they spent their money. It drove him crazy and made him think horrible thoughts about her and her boring need to justify the numbers. "Henry is a clever man."

Arlo stood in the shower and as the steam gathered and fogged up the glass shower door he laughed and traced a heart. He then put his initials at the top of the heart. He stood there for several moments, hesitating in what to write next. *Go on*, he urged, *who is ever going to know?* He traced the letters E.C on the screen. It shocked him that he had not even considered one of the three women he was currently dating. *It's just that you have spent the whole day with her*, he reassured himself. He swiped his hand across the love heart and turned off the shower.

Briskly he dried himself and pulled on a pair of jeans and a light t-shirt. It was going to be a warm night and if he was going to take in a few sights he wanted to be comfortable. He had no one to impress, so jeans it was. Arlo dried his hair and ran his fingers through it, allowing the short waves to sit however they wanted. He was keen to get out there and explore LA a little.

The elevators opened to reveal Emersyn standing in the middle of the hotel lobby. Jeans and t-shirt on and hair pulled up in a high, slick ponytail. "Hi." she smiled as he exited the lift.

"Hi," he hesitated, "are you joining your friend again tonight?"

She frowned. "My friend?"

"Yeah, tall, dark, and rich in the bar last night."

"Oh, Jeremy. We went to Notre Dame together," Emersyn said airily. "You almost sound jealous."

Arlo ignored the jibe. "So not meeting Jeremy tonight?"

"No. I thought I might head out and take in some sights. It has been a long time since I was here last."

"That's what I was planning on doing, would you care to join me?" The words were out of his mouth before he had thought through the question.

Emersyn looked grateful. "That would be amazing. There is a lot of crazy out there and I wasn't looking forward to dealing with it on my own. Maybe we can get a bite to eat too? I'm starving."

Arlo fought the want to take her hand and walked with her out the hotel doors. "Something to eat would be great. What is at the top of your list to visit?"

⸻ ◦ ⸻

"I'll have the spaghetti marinara and garlic bread, please?" Emersyn ordered.

"And you, Sir?"

"That sounds great, I'll have the same, thanks."

Arlo was tired, but quietly content. He had spent the last several hours traipsing around LA with Emersyn and it had not been weird or uncomfortable. She had made a great travel companion and had been excited to participate in anything he chose to see. Now they sat, crowd watching, on the boardwalk of Venice Beach. The cute, tiny Italian restaurant had large wooden shutters that were thrown open to allow patrons to experience the entertainment that was on offer.

"Are you nervous about tomorrow?" Emersyn asked.

Arlo thought about it. "I am, I always am when I have to present to a new client. So much is riding on it and in the end, it rests completely on my shoulders and what I chose to go with." He took a sip of the red wine he ordered and then grinned at her. "I was terrified when I had to answer to you and present to you that I had prepared after that first meeting."

Emersyn chuckled. "Am I truly that scary?"

"In your boss accountant mode?" he raised his eyebrows at her. "Hell, yeah."

"Good! I worked hard to be that intimidating." She winked at him.

Arlo laughed but wasn't quite sure if she was serious or not. He was saved from commenting further by the arrival of their meals. They ate in silence for a while, watching the magician that was performing on stilts at the front of the restaurant window.

"You were talking about Notre Dame on the plane, did you consider going anywhere else?" Arlo began the conversation. This was what he was great at, getting women to talk and he felt like he knew nothing about Emersyn. She had opened up on the plane about her terrible marriage for a moment but had stopped at telling him anything truly personal.

"No, not really. I was living in New York at the time and Notre Dame was prestigious enough for me and far enough away from home." She continued to watch the street performer.

Well, that was enlightening, yet completely uninformative at the same time. Neat trick, he thought.

"What about you? Why did you choose the University of Texas?"

"They offered me a partial scholarship," he paused and considered his next words carefully. Should he tell her the truth? For unknown reasons, it was important to him for Emersyn to see him in a good light. "I told my parents it was a full scholarship, so they didn't have to pay for my tuition. They had worked so hard and sacrificed so much to send us to good schools, that I just couldn't take their money when I no longer needed to."

"I don't know what to say. That is something not many people do. Have you ever told your parents?"

"No, I paid off the tuition fees in my third year at the firm. I got a great bonus when I was given my current role. I don't see the point in telling them. They will feel bad for no reason. I am hoping they use the money they had saved and go back to Spain to visit my Dad's family. They talk about it, but never do it."

"Why do you think they never do it?" Emersyn asked.

Arlo shrugged. "I don't know. Dad makes excuses that there is no one to run the business, but they have great staff who are quite capable of selling farm equipment." He gazed out the window, past the crowds, and watched the waves roll onto the dirty sand of the fabled Venice Beach. "I should ask them."

"Life is too short to wait for things you want. Once we know what we want, we should always take time to do them." Emersyn spoke quietly.

Arlo turned his head back to her and was again caught by her beauty. "The trick is to figure out what we want."

Chapter 12

The sound of the treadmill, her feet hitting the belt and her labored breathing filled the small gym on the top floor of the hotel. Her thighs protested as Emersyn increased the incline on the machine. *Don't blame me*, she muttered, *it was your idea to eat all those carbs last night.* She attempted to enjoy the view but her mind wandered and she was back in the hotel corridor last night with Arlo.

He had walked her to her room and they had stood at the door, an awkward silence growing between them. It was the first time she had felt anything akin to attraction on more than just a physical level since her heart had been shattered by Nicolai and it unsettled her. Arlo wasn't the person she thought he was. Oh, he was still arrogant and untrustworthy, but weren't all men? No matter how much she wanted to believe that he would always be honest with her, she found it difficult to trust in that. Yet, he had shown her kindness, fun, and a willingness to let her see his vulnerable side when he spoke about his family.

They had stood there for several moments before he had smiled in his charming way and shrugged his shoulders as if he had come to a decision. "Well, it was wonderful to see LA with you. Hopefully, when we get back to Austin you will trust me to play tour guide and I can show you more than just the places Jaya has been taking you."

"Maybe," Emersyn was noncommittal. She liked the idea of seeing more of the place she was now calling home, but to explore it with Arlo was perhaps not the best idea.

Jaya's words kept swirling in her head. *He doesn't sleep with people he works with.* If that were true, she could take him up on the offer. She would have to wait a little longer to see, eventually, everyone always showed their true colors.

"I had a great night. Thanks for letting me tag along."

"I'll meet you in the conference room at 9:00 am." Arlo turned and walked away. "Sweet dreams," he called over his shoulder.

"You too," she had called back and then thought how stupid that sounded and had hurried to get her door open.

Emersyn pushed the button on the treadmill and it slowed to a crawl, before turning off. She looked at her phone as she grabbed a towel and realized that she didn't have that long until she had to meet Arlo. In record time she had showered, changed, done her hair, and applied minimal make-up to arrive five minutes early. This gave her the chance to again triple check her spreadsheets before the presentation today. Everything had to be perfect.

Her phone dinged and it was a message from Jaya. **Good luck today. You got this. Just sit back and enjoy the brilliance of Arlo. You'll get to see why the company puts up with the revolving secretaries. ;-)**

Emersyn giggled to herself. **It has been an educational trip. I can already see why they allow the reassignment of secretaries on an annual basis. You don't need to tell him this, but I am in awe of his ability to get this all together so quickly. Gtg xox**

She put her phone down and returned to the laptop screen as he walked in.

"Already hard at work, I see. Are you ready?" he asked cheerfully.

"Sure, my job is easy for now. Keeping you on budget might be more of a challenge later. This is your show this afternoon, I am just here for the ride." She stood and closed her laptop. Emersyn smoothed down the front skirt section of her pouf style dress. She loved the swirls in different shades of ochre that the material showcased perfectly.

They both began to pack up the presentation. Going through the checklist that Arlo had created and making sure everything was in order. An hour later found them standing out the front of the hotel. Arlo carrying a large portfolio and Emersyn holding the box that contained the Happy Girl hair care line they had received at the first meeting.

As the company hired car pulled in Emersyn spoke quietly to Arlo. "Good luck today. Whatever happens, I am impressed with the campaign and will now officially get off your case when we get back."

❖

Arlo

Arlo adjusted his tie as he stood at the front of the hotel waiting for Emersyn and the hire car. He was buoyant with the afternoon's presentation and subsequent acceptance email and offer for celebratory dinner with the team at Happy Girl. The Concierge came out and handed him a folded piece of paper. It was a note from Emersyn.

Hi Arlo,

Sorry, but I have developed a migraine. If I don't get to bed when they start, they last for days. Please go and enjoy your evening. You deserve all the accolades from the presentation this afternoon.

I have let Michael and Tiffany know that I won't be attending so you won't need to worry about their reaction when you turn up alone.

Again, congratulations,

Emersyn.

He folded the paper and put it in his pocket. "Damn." He swore to himself.

The car pulled up and he climbed in. Arlo took out his phone and sent a quick text to Emersyn in response to her message. **Hey, sorry to hear you are feeling unwell. If there is anything I can pick you up while am out please let me know. I wish you were celebrating with us. Without your original shower confession, the rest would not have happened. Get some rest, Arlo.**

He looked at the text and hesitated. Did he finish with a smiley face or a sad face? Or did he do a couple of xox? The etiquette of texting still eluded him at times. He decided not to add anything and hit send.

Quickly they arrived at the beautiful restaurant Michael had chosen to celebrate their venture at. It was decorated with old fashion panache, all deep red furnishings with hints of gold. It would be a beautiful place to shoot a commercial in, Arlo noted. He was escorted to the table to discover all the people that had been at the original meeting and today's presentation were in attendance. He greeted everyone with a wave but took the time to shake Michael and Tiffany's hands.

Arlo found himself seated between Tiffany and the hot marketing manager Pascal. He greeted Pascal with a warm smile and in return felt his leg squeezed gently by a hand on his thigh. "I am glad you could make it. I wanted to ask you a few questions about marketing and your thoughts on current trends."

"Sure, I am happy to talk shop. Just as long you understand I can't give away trade secrets." He winked at her and she laughed.

Tiffany inserted herself into the conversation. "That sounds fabulous. I have questions too. There are a few things that they are teaching us that just aren't clear to me why we bother."

Michael spoke over the top of them. "Ladies, let the man breathe. Allow him to at least order a drink before you pounce on him."

Everyone at the table laughed and Arlo ordered Scotch on the rocks before he was bombarded with more questions. He tried to include everyone in the conversation, as it served no purpose to get anyone offside when he had to work with these people for the next six months.

The night flew by, with dinner being a delicious blend of Asian and Indian cuisines. A few people ordered dessert and Arlo thought about taking something back for Emersyn but didn't think sweet food would be good for a migraine.

The evening finally wound down and while Arlo had a late morning flight the rest all had work to get up to.

Arlo shook Michael's hand as they both stood. "Thank you again, for this marvellous opportunity. I am sorry that Emersyn couldn't make it tonight."

"So am I, she is a great asset to your company, with a gift for numbers. I look forward to working with both of you."

"And I look forward to working with both of you when I can too. I get the feeling I can learn a lot just watching you two work together. You make a great team." Tiffany shook his hand after her father had released it.

"I don't think I'm ready to wrap up yet. One more drink in celebration before I head back to the hotel." Arlo looked around at the table of people, who were all getting ready to leave. "Anyone care to join me?" he asked casually, almost certain at the response he would get.

"Oh, I will stay and keep you company," Pascal answered sweetly. "One more drink won't hurt anyone."

Chapter 13

Emersyn

Her laptop lay open on the round table, the screen on the same email it had been on from the night before. Her hands shook as she took a sip of her morning's coffee. Could this be happening again? Another email, just like the one sent that destroyed her marriage. *To be fair an email didn't destroy your marriage, your asshole husband did that.*

Would Nicolai and his choices ever stop haunting her? She felt sick.

Emersyn had returned from the successful presentation yesterday afternoon to spend a fabulous hour lazing by the hotel pool, reading a new serial killer novel, and sipping on a delicious fresh fruit cocktail. She had watched Arlo walk through the lobby and head to the bar. He turned his head in her direction at one point and she ducked her head and pretended to be engrossed in her book. She did not feel like company and the need to keep her guard up around him. He was clever and knew how to make you feel like he heard what you said and understood you, it was disarming and she had no intention of falling for it.

"Hi," a figure had cast a long shadow across her sun lounge and intruded on her reading.

She ignored the male voice hoping, it would go away.

"Hello?"

Emersyn gave in and looked up into the wrinkled eyes of a middle-aged man with a potbelly covered in matted, graying hair. She refrained from shuddering. "Hi."

"Can I buy you a drink?"

"No, thanks, I have one." She pointed to the umbrella laden cocktail, attempting to keep her voice light.

"Oh, come on. A pretty girl like you shouldn't be out here alone."

"Why?" she asked. This was her favorite part of dealing with morons that chose to interrupt her and then not accept no.

"Why what?" he asked. His creased, saggy brow frowned with confusion.

"Why shouldn't I be alone?"

"I'm sorry?" his voice became less sure.

"Oh, don't be sorry."

"Huh?"

"You were apologizing for interrupting me," she answered sweetly.

"I was?"

"You weren't?"

"Ah, okay. I'll be going now."

"Bye," Emersyn smiled innocently. She took a satisfying sip of her drink as he watched the man waddle away.

"Oh, that was priceless." Arlo applauded as he walked over and plonked down on the chair next to her.

Emersyn bowed slightly. "Thank you. I don't mind being approached by a man. It takes guts, but when I decline their offer, they need to be gracious and leave again."

"Well, I didn't mean to interrupt your 'me' time, but I thought you might like to know that our proposal has been accepted and we have been invited out to a celebration dinner with the Happy Girl people."

Arlo was beaming. He raised his glass to her. "Congratulations. We did it."

"You did it. I just made impressive-looking spreadsheets and helped with the original idea." She clinked her glass against his. "What time is dinner?"

"The car is picking us up at 7:00 pm."

She looked at her phone and noted she had several emails. Probably about the proposal acceptance. "I better get back to the room then, if we are leaving in an hour." She stood and wrapped the hotel towel around herself. "I'll meet you out the front."

Her restful afternoon had come to an abrupt end once she had gotten back to her hotel room and opened her emails. The first email had been the confirmation email and invitation. The second email explained that the next step in the process would be contracts that would be emailed and signed the following day. The third email had brought back pain, betrayal, and bitterness that she thought she had moved through.

Emersyn finished her coffee and quickly packed her suitcases. All the while her laptop stood open, the email displayed. Should she ignore it? Should she contact her lawyer? She thought about the email telling Emersyn that it's all her fault that her daughter can't eat. That when Emersyn ran off with all the money, Nicolai had stopped giving them money. What had her ex told the woman? And what was she supposed to do? Emersyn felt horrible that if it were true the child was not eating but did the trollop who slept with her husband expect sympathy from the woman she betrayed?

The thought of sitting in a room full of people and being cheerful when her past had caught up with her seemed impossible, so Emersyn decided to feign a migraine. She had slept poorly as the email from the mistress played on her mind.

As Emersyn zipped up her garment bag and put on her heels her laptop pinged. Another email had come through. She rushed to it in the hope that it was good news that the contracts were signed and completed.

She quickly read the email and almost screamed in frustration. What the hell had he done last night?

———◦◦———

Arlo

It didn't take long for Arlo to pack his suitcase and place it near the door. He hummed happily to himself as he double-checked all the usual places things fell behind or under in a hotel room, to make sure he had collected everything. His stomach growled loudly; it was time for breakfast. *I wonder if I should text Emersyn to find out if she feels better and wants me to bring up anything for breakfast?*

Before he had decided his phone began to ring. It was his mom. "Hi Mom, how are you?"

"I am great. I have your father on loudspeaker."

"Hi Papa," Arlo added.

"Hi." His father never spoke much on the phone, but in person you couldn't keep him quiet.

His mother took control of the conversation. "We couldn't wait any longer and didn't know what time your flight was. How did the big presentation go yesterday?"

"Oh, Mom, it went perfectly. Emersyn came up with this great idea and once we had that everything else just fell into place. Happy Girl loved it all and we got the acceptance last night. The contracts will be emailed and signed today while we fly home and I will hand it over to the team to start working on on Monday."

"You give it over to someone else?" his mother sounded confused.

"Yes, Mum. I don't do all the work myself. I come up with a concept, with everyone's help develop it, make sure that accounts approve it, pitch it and then hand it over to my team."

"But it was your idea, don't you want to see it followed through?"

Arlo laughed. It didn't matter how many times he explained it, she just didn't understand. "I do follow it through. They report everything to me and I make all final decisions. Then I have to get Emersyn to approve it and we are good to launch once the client sees the finished product."

"Who is Emersyn?" His father interrupted. "You have said her name several times now."

"Emersyn is the woman I am here with. She is the new head of marketing accounting and she's incredible. Her spreadsheets were the envy of the accounting team at Happy Girl."

"You like her?" His mother sounded hopeful for the wrong reasons.

"Yes, I like her. She pushes me. I got lazy and she called me on it. I didn't like it much, you know me, but I sucked it up and now I have found my passion again." He didn't like admitting that he had been putting in half the effort he used to. It had been wonderful to rediscover his drive. "She works hard and is professional and expects the same from everyone she works with."

"I like her already." His mother announced.

"Mom, I gotta go or I am going to miss breakfast."

"Go, go. I don't want you fading away. Love you and let me know when you are home. I don't like it when you fly."

"Bye, Son."

"See you, love you both." He hung before they could go on.

He grabbed his wallet and room card off the table and opened the door to head to breakfast to find Emersyn standing there, her hand raised to knock. Her usually beautiful face was contorted with rage and her green eyes bore into him. "What were you thinking?" her voice trembled with anger as she fought for control of her temper.

Chapter 14

Arlo looked shocked as she glared at him. "I'm waiting?" she prompted.

"I am completely confused. What are you talking about?"

"Have you not checked your emails in the last half hour?" she managed to ask through her clenched teeth.

"No, I have been packing." He looked like he had swallowed something foul as he finally started to comprehend that something was wrong. "What's happened?"

"I'd read your emails," she hissed. She couldn't believe how stupid he had been. Putting everything in jeopardy just to get a girl into bed. "I'll wait."

Quickly, he pulled out his phone and opened the email. Emersyn watched as the color drained from his normally tanned face. "I don't understand. What do they mean they have reconsidered and are now choosing to decline the proposal?" He ran his hand through his hair and looked up at her. "Why do you think it is my fault?"

Emersyn ground her teeth together. "Because Pascal is married to Michael Bowen's best friend, you idiot."

"Pascal is married? She never mentioned that last night."

"She didn't?" Emersyn was skeptical. "I have a meeting with Michael in half an hour. I'm leaving now."

"I'll come with you," he offered.

"You will do no such thing. You will go have breakfast, do the checkout, and wait for me to return. If I am not back in time just head to the airport; I will meet you there if necessary." She was furious with him. Arlo went to say something, but she held up her hand. "Try not to sleep with anyone while I'm gone."

"Thank you for seeing me, Michael." Emersyn shook his hand and sat in the indicated seat across the desk from the CEO of Happy Girl.

"I'm not sure why you would want to see me. I thought I had made it clear in the email and subsequent phone call that we wouldn't be moving forward with Chalmers and Tran," Michael reiterated. His gray eyes serious.

There was a polite knock on the door, but the knocker didn't wait to be invited in, they simply opened the door. Tiffany entered and softly closed the door behind her.

"You are supposed to be on a plane," Michael told his daughter gruffly.

"And you aren't supposed to make important decisions without me." Her gaze was piercing as she adjusted her soft pink, high waisted crepe trousers before she sat. They complimented the pale gray halter neck top she wore that matched her gray eyes, which were so like her father's. Soft gray leather gladiator sandals with a wedge heel completed the look. "Now," she turned to Emersyn, "what happened?"

"I'm not sure. I spoke to Arlo this morning and he assures me that he had no idea she was married."

"They were flirting last night at dinner." Michael spoke before anyone else could. "Tiff, you were there, it was obvious."

"Dad, if it was that obvious why didn't you say something? She is your best friend's wife, after all, that is why we are sitting here." She turned back to Emersyn. "Yes, they were flirting, but Pascal is married so I didn't think anything of it."

Emersyn finally spoke. "May I be so bold as to ask why you are allowing your best friend to interfere with a good business decision?"

Silence hung in the room and everyone looked uncomfortable. Tiffany was the one to finally end it by looking at her father with regret and spoke softly. "Sorry, Daddy."

Michael stared at his daughter, but didn't respond.

"Mom cheated on Dad and ran off with our home chef." Her voice was small and sad. "As you can imagine, cheating is vile and completely unacceptable in our house." Tears shone in her eyes, but she maintained her composure. "She abandoned all of us that day."

"I am so sorry to hear that and I completely agree." Emersyn took a steadying breath and decided that if she needed to reveal her own pain to get this fixed, she would. "My husband cheated on me and I was completely oblivious to it until I was emailed photos of his child." Her voice was wooden, emotionless. Her pain well-buried. "What happened last night was completely wrong, but not on Arlo's part. He is not married. He did not know Pascal was married. This is Pascal's doing, not his." She looked to Michael. "Your employee put her desires above your company's success. Punishing us will not absolve that."

She changed tack and turned to Tiffany. "You have worked too hard to allow this to not go forward. You and I both know this campaign will take you next level in global branding, but it is our idea until the dotted line is signed. Do you want us to take this idea elsewhere?" She knew it was a risk to push that hard, but could sense both wanted the right thing for the company. Michael had reacted emotionally and she wanted to give him a chance to see it and an out of the situation he had created.

Father and daughter sat staring at each other. Emersyn now turned to Michael and appealed to the businessman rather than the emotions for the best friend. "You and I both know that there are no friends in business. Would this best friend walk away from the potential this deal has for you if he were in the same position?"

<hr />

Arlo

Deep breaths. Just take deep breaths, Arlo told himself as he waited at the boarding gate for their flight back to Austin. He felt wretched for destroying a lucrative contract, yet underneath, he was confused as to how this had become his fault. Pascal had made her needs and intentions clear and there had never been a mention of a husband. Was he supposed to ask if she was married? Wasn't the onus on the person who was married to not cheat?

He found cheating repulsive; who hadn't had their heart broken by someone sneaking around behind their back? He didn't cheat. A little voice spoke up. *How could you cheat when you don't commit? Oh, shut up,* he told it.

Arlo stood at the humungous glass windows that allowed travelers to see the comings and goings of the planes on the tarmac. Usually, this didn't interest him, but today he tried to find distraction. There was a polite cough behind him and he spun, expecting to see Emersyn; instead, he was faced with the pretty, young Tiffany. "Tiffany, I am so sorry. You have to believe me when I tell you that I didn't know she was married," he pleaded his case.

Tiffany smiled kindly. "I know exactly what type of person Pascal is, but Dad and his buddy are blind to it. The sooner I get this degree completed, the sooner she can be gone and I can take the reins. I am on my way back to school now. Emersyn and I caught a cab here together, she has just got a longer cue at her airline check-in."

"And?" he prompted. Was Tiffany aware that she hadn't told him the result of the meeting?

"Congratulations. Thanks to Emersyn and her persuasive arguments, the contracts have been signed and emailed to your office." Tiffany shook his hand. "I look forward to working with you, as I think Dad will keep Pascal away from the launch now. Great for me. If I'm smart, I can work it all into my final assessment." Tiffany leaned in close to Arlo. "Next time you need company, maybe ask me instead." She winked at him, giggled in the way only college girls giggle, and strode off.

Arlo watched her walk away. Relief flooded his thoughts as what Tiffany had just told him sunk in. How had Emersyn done it?

The flight attendant at the gate announced that they could start boarding and he made his way to the line to find Emersyn waiting there. "Hi," he said as he stopped behind her.

"Hello." Her response was chilly at best.

"Thank you, I owe you one."

"You don't owe me anything. I did it because it had to be done."

"How did you fix it?"

"Tiffany helped. I noticed she wasn't on the original email this morning, so I contacted her. She delayed her departure and between us, we managed to convince her father that moving forward with our proposal was in the best interests of Happy Girl."

They moved through the gate and started down the corridor to the plane. Emersyn tried to walk ahead of him. Why was she being so hostile?

"What can I do to make this right?"

She glared at him. "I don't know why men think it is okay to sleep with anyone they fancy and have the hubris to believe there will never be consequences." She moved onto the plane and headed towards her seat.

Arlo followed her. "That's not fair. What I do on my time is my business."

"You made it everyone's business when you couldn't control your libido—or is it ego?—for the few short days we were away." Emersyn handed over her garment bag and threw her carry-on luggage on to the seat he was about to sit in. "I think you will find you are not sitting here."

He checked his ticket to discover that he wasn't sitting next to her on the flight home. They were diagonally positioned in the cabin. Arlo was stunned; she had gone as far as to request she sit away from him. "Emersyn?"

"Stay away from me, Arlo. I thought I had misunderstood you, but it turns out I was spot on. You need to think about what sort of person you want the world to see you as."

Arlo swallowed hard around the bitter taste in his mouth and moved to find his seat. *How am I going to get her to trust me now? And why was it so damn important that she did?*

Chapter 15

Emersyn

Cool water splashed on her bare legs as a child giggling could be heard. Emersyn feigned sleep as she cranked her eyelid open a fraction—hidden behind her sunglasses—and watched Eddie, Harvey's eldest grandchild, sneak closer to her with the encouragement of his father, Leighton. There was much whispering and hushing going on as he was urged to creep forward, a small water pistol in his tiny hand. What neither of them knew was that Emersyn had been tipped off that this had been in the planning all week while she was away in LA. On the way home from the airport on late Friday afternoon, she had made one quick stop at a toy shop and had picked up the biggest water gun she could find. That Saturday morning Harvey had placed it next to her chair and covered it with a towel when he had set up the lounges by the pool while everyone had gone to their rooms to change into their bathing suits.

Emersyn's hand rested on the concealed weapon and she figured a few more steps and both of these mischief makers were going to get saturated. A light spray of mist covered her torso as Eddie's little fingers struggled to pull the slippery trigger. It was perfect timing as Leighton bent to help his son and now they were both occupied. Grabbing the water gun, Emersyn aimed and pulled the trigger, keeping her finger down and a wonderful, long consistent stream of cold water covered them both. Leighton, in true dad style, picked up Eddie and held him out like a shield and they backed up as Emersyn stood and advanced on the naughty pair.

Everyone joined in the laughter as Leighton called out to his wife, Darcey, Harvey's eldest daughter, to save them. "Help us, please? Look at her attacking your firstborn."

Laughing Darcey marched over to Emersyn and stood in between them, facing her. "I must insist that you stop shooting at my son."

Emersyn continued to move forward but had ceased shooting until she came to stand directly before Darcey who took the water pistol that Emersyn surreptitiously handed her.

"Okay, I'll stop now. But I have something to admit," Emersyn declared.

"What?" Leighton asked suspiciously.

Darcey winked at Emersyn, who raised both hands to reveal they were empty. "I don't have it anymore."

Darcey opened fire on her husband and child, who both squealed and laughed as she edged them closer to the pool. "Surrender my son and I will spare him," ordered Darcey.

Leighton laughed and put down their child, who went rushing to his Auntie Pippa's chair and climbed into her lap, as his Grandpa's lap was taken up with his sleepy baby sister, Athena. At that moment the water pistol ran out of ammunition and Darcey shrieked with laughter as Leighton advanced on her. He still held the small gun that had started the whole thing. Darcey ran from her husband and was greeted with a chorus of adult voices reminding her, "No running," as they had spent the last several hours telling Eddie to not run around the pool area.

"Oops, sorry," she called and slowed to a brisk walk. Leighton, with his much longer legs, swiftly caught up to her and discarded his empty pistol; instead, he grabbed his wife and threatened to toss her into the pool. "You wouldn't do that to me."

Leighton smirked and pretended to hover over the edge. "Really? You sure about that?"

Darcey looked confident as she continued to struggle against her husband. "Yes, you wouldn't throw a pregnant lady in the pool."

He let go and looked at her. "Really?"

"Yes," she said with a laugh, as she took advantage of his shock and gave him a firm shove that sent him into the water.

He came up spluttering while everyone gathered around Darcey to congratulate her. "Why didn't you tell me?" Leighton asked as he hauled himself out the side of the pool.

"I was waiting for the right time and this just presented itself so perfectly." Darcey grinned at him.

He wrapped her up in his wet arms and she squealed in protest. "You're wet!"

"Oh hush, I'm trying to kiss you." Leighton finally congratulated his wife with a big, wet kiss before he shook his curly light brown hair and sprayed her with water like a shaggy dog.

Everyone was hit with the droplets and took several steps back. "Ewwww."

"I'm going to take this one up for her nap," announced Harvey, who held his granddaughter like she was the finest china. All the raucous laughter had not made Athena more alert; she continued to snuggle into his arms.

Leighton wrapped a yellow and white striped pool towel around his waist and picked up Eddie. "This one needs a little quiet time too, or by dinner he is going to be difficult." He gently kissed the top of the little boy's head. "Daddy is going to read you a story."

"Peter Pan," announced Eddie.

"Peter Pan it is," agreed Leighton.

As the three women refilled their drinks and lie back down on their sun lounges, Emersyn winked at Darcey. "Thank you for the heads up about the water pistol, I think it worked out quite well."

"You told her what they were planning?" Pippa asked astounded.

Darcey nodded with a tiny satisfied smile. "Us girls have got to stick together. And it was fun watching all those plans crumble around Leighton."

As Emersyn settled into her lounge and took a sip of the delicious Sangria Harvey had whipped up, she tried not to think of the Spanish man that made her heart race in a way it hadn't for a long time. Their time together had been wonderful. He was exceptional at his job and gifted with knowing what to do with a single idea. You can't learn that. And just as she had begun to change her mind about his womanizing ways, he slept with the first person that paid him attention, regardless of how professional it looked. Emersyn was furious with him and still didn't know how she was going to deal with him at work on Monday. He had seemed genuine in his want to apologize, yet kept trying to blame Pascal or his own choices. Why do men never take responsibility for their shit?

"What do you think, Emersyn?" asked Pippa.

"Huh? Sorry, was off with the fairies. It has been a long week," Emersyn apologized.

"I was saying that Dad seems to be happier and more back to his normal self," Darcey said.

"And I agreed. He appears to be with us again and engaged with what's happening, rather than just putting on a brave face," Pippa explained. "What do you think? You are the one that lives with him."

"I think he still misses your mom terribly, but each day brings him new joy. Harvey loves you girls, and watching you achieve everything he and Selena had both hoped for you makes him proud."

Pippa sniffed; she was always the most sentimental. "Now you have made me cry."

"Okay, let's change the subject," announced Darcey. "Which do you like better? Peter Pan or Little Mermaid."

Chapter 16

Arlo

"Jaya, do you think that she will ever forgive me?" Arlo asked quietly as he watched Emersyn hurry away. It had been two weeks since they had returned from LA and every time Emersyn encountered Arlo, she made an excuse to leave or just turned around and walked away, as she had just done.

Jaya followed Arlo's gaze. "I don't know. I'm not even sure she knows why she is so angry at you." Jaya gave him a calculating look. "I would never break her confidence and I am guessing, but her trust issues run deep and you showed her that…well, I don't understand what she thinks you showed her." Jaya shrugged. "I'm not that much help." She did give him her own exasperated look. "I have been good about not saying anything, but since you brought it up… What on Earth were you thinking?"

Arlo put his hands up in surrender. "I don't know how many more times I can say that I didn't know she was married."

"So?" Jaya looked scornful. "I think in essence that is the problem. Just because you thought she wasn't married, you believe it excuses you for sleeping with someone from a company you are going to be working closely with? What happens if she went all stalkerish, or people started to think we got the contract because you slept with the marketing manager? There are at least another five scenarios I can think of where it ends badly."

"I didn't think of anything other than she was a gorgeous woman who wanted to do a little celebrating with me," Arlo admitted. "Shit. I really messed up."

"Ah, hello. What, you just figured out you almost lost the contract? Emersyn saved your job, as well as the contract... and you still keep behaving like you have nothing to apologize for because the woman didn't tell you she was married." Jaya rolled her eyes at him.

"So, I'm a bigger idiot than I thought," Arlo stated.

"It would appear so." Jaya smiled. "But, I still wouldn't work for anyone else."

"Thank you... I think."

"She will be waiting for me downstairs. I'm off to lunch; I'll see you in an hour." Jaya waved airily as she walked off in the direction Emersyn had gone.

Arlo went back into his office and closed the door behind him. He lied down on the couch and put his arm over his face as the sun streamed in through the tenth-floor office window. "Shit. I can't believe I have made such a mess of this. How did I miss that?" he wondered aloud.

He lie still, feeling sorry for himself and finally coming to understand that no matter what light you put it in, he shouldn't have slept with Pascal. He wondered, not for the first time, exactly what Emersyn had said to save the situation.

Arlo wanted to talk to Emersyn. He wanted her to know how much he had enjoyed working with her and how he admired her ability and determination to get the best out of everyone, even when they were obstinate like he had been.

His musings were interrupted by a polite knock on the door. "Yes?" he called.

Eva, the secretary, opened the door and poked her head in. "Sorry to disturb you. I can't find Jaya and just needed a yes or no on an email I had to send." She waved a piece of paper at him. "I printed it off for you to look at." She came into the office and passed it to him. "Are you feeling okay?"

Arlo groaned as he took his arm from his eyes and sat up. "Just a hint of a headache."

"I can give you a neck massage if you like?" offered Eva. She wiggled her slender fingers at him.

Arlo was tempted. "That would be great but could be very easily misconstrued if someone walked in." He put his glasses on and went over the paper she had handed him. "This seems all in order. Email away." He handed the paper back to her.

"Thanks. Let me know if you ever want that message." Eva breezed back out the door.

What was it with women this month? He had several make him obvious offers and the one that he wanted to get to know continually hid from him. He lie back and re-covered his eyes. Emersyn's stunning green eyes and beautiful face filled his mind.

—◦◦◦—

Emersyn

Emersyn and Jaya settled into their chairs. Emersyn was grateful to have a rotating fan blow air onto her back. "So, what took you so long?"

"You know what took me so long. You saw me standing with Arlo when you walked down the corridor before you did the most obvious about face and scurried back to the elevator."

"I did not scurry." Emersyn was indignant. "I simply realized that I needed to use the restroom before we left."

"Yeah, okay." Jaya didn't look convinced. "He wanted to know when you are going to talk to him."

"I do talk to him."

"Barely. Most of it is done via email or through me or Mrs. Beulieu," Jaya pointed out.

"He is a busy man. I don't wish to disturb him."

Jaya looked directly at her, making Emersyn slightly uncomfortable with the straightforwardness of the stare. "What?" Emersyn asked.

"You like him," Jaya stated.

"You're crazy."

"Don't deflect." Jaya's eyes narrowed. "He says you had a great time in LA and worked well together. You saw another side to him."

"I saw the side he shows all his dates to get them in bed." Emersyn scoffed. "He's a womanizer. He knows exactly what to say and asks a lot of questions to get you to talk." She didn't add that he had talked about himself and revealed private experiences and information. Far more than Emersyn had. Arlo had asked questions and she had answered to a point and then deflected to him because she was uncomfortable. He had been open and honest... her thoughts darkened... maybe that was his thing. Jaya had told her that he was always honest.

"Hello, are you listening to me or daydreaming about Arlo?" Jaya intruded on her thoughts.

Emersyn thankfully didn't blush. "I was thinking what I should have for lunch."

"A lot of this could have been avoided if you didn't get that stupid migraine."

"Okay, so now it is my fault?"

"No, Arlo is a grown man and makes his own choices, and boy, that choice was dumb. But if you had have been there, he would have never have considered going home with Pascal."

"You don't know that."

"I know he likes you."

Emersyn didn't want to think about it. At the moment, there were many things she didn't want to think about. The email that had made her miss that fateful celebration dinner still sat unanswered in her inbox. She had thought about telling Jaya the whole sordid story but just couldn't find the words to start.

Emersyn was saved from commenting by the waitress asking if they were ready to order. After she had placed her order and taken a sip of the iced tea she had been given, she changed the subject. "What do you think about me offering to host a party at my place to celebrate the acquisition of the Happy Girl account? It gives me a chance to meet more people from the office and people can bring their partners if they want to."

"Yes, that sounds wonderful. I am always up for a party and would love to see your place." Jaya clapped her hands in excitement. "Let's hope Mr. Tran goes for the idea."

Chapter 17

Emersyn

Emersyn was coming down the stairs as Harvey opened the door in response to the heavy donging of the fancy doorbell. She got to the bottom of the sweeping curved staircase in time to hear Jaya introduce herself. There were people everywhere as Harvey showed Jaya in. "Wow, there is a lot going on here. Looks like someone is having a party," Jaya joked as she hugged Emersyn hello.

The party company that had been hired to cater the event had started their preparations yesterday; moving the furniture out of the large lounge room, dining room, and makeshift theatre room Emersyn had had set up when she moved in. The theatre room had originally been her father's game room, filled with a billiard table and a beautifully crafted chess table that no one had ever used. As well as a bar that could seat twelve people, an air hockey table, and several lounges and chairs placed so you could see the TVs, one for each wall. It now made the perfect theatre room, as it had minimal windows and bi-fold doors in the center of a wall that led to the spacious dining room, which usually housed a table that could comfortably seat twenty-four people, with room to spare.

The dining room had floor to ceiling windows and glass sliding doors that opened onto a balcony that could be accessed by the lounge room next door as well. The balcony looked over the perfectly manicured gardens and half of the sparkling blue pool below that was her mother's legacy to the estate. Emersyn's mother had loved to garden, but as she got sicker she found it taxing, so she would create gardens that Emersyn's father would have to build. The garden would always have a special picnic spot. This house's special picnic spot could not be viewed from the balcony.

The theatre room had been turned into what could only be described as a mini nightclub. Strobe lights were being fitted and a fog machine was placed in a corner. The large bar her father had built was still there, but with gleaming new chrome chairs to match the overall party color theme of black and chrome with hints of bubble-gum pink—to tie in the Happy Girl celebration—while the dining room was left bare, with a minimal number of chairs set around for those who needed to rest. Another small bar had been set up in the area, with a third one set up in the lounge. Her lounge chairs, with more brought in, had been rearranged for people to gather in seated groups that wanted to be the furthest from the music and dance floor.

This morning had seen the events people come back with the decorations, floating lights for the pool, extra lights for the driveway, and the DJ equipment. Amongst all this, the caterers were in the kitchen, whipping up delectable treats from all corners of the globe. Rather than one food theme, Emersyn had chosen to go global and incorporate finger food from every continent.

"Come on, let's get out of this chaos." Emersyn looked to Jaya, who carried more than one garment bag. "I see you brought a few dresses. Couldn't make up your mind?"

"You have no idea."

"Do you want something to eat or drink?"

"Yes, please." Jaya smiled.

"Harvey, can you please send up a platter and some champagne? Oh, and Lydia, the make-up artist should be here any minute. Please show her up when she arrives."

Emersyn led the way up the marble stairs, with Jaya oohing and aahing as they went along. "I don't mean to sound rude, but this is your house?"

"No, it's my dad's. He made his money flipping houses before it was a thing, and then when he married Mom, he kept every house they had lived in. The ones we don't use are being rented out."

"It's gorgeous. I love the mix between classic and modern. And the warm tones are just beautiful."

"Mom had excellent taste." Emersyn led her to the suite that was her bedroom.

"Holy shit." Jaya laughed as they entered her room. "So, this is the master bedroom?"

"No, this is my room when I was much younger. Mom never knew how long she wanted to stay anywhere and always made sure my room was large enough that I could grow into it. Half of what is now my closet was once a toy room."

Emersyn opened the double closet doors and watched Jaya swoon. "What until you see the bathroom."

"Oh, I'm not sure I can handle any more of this extravagance." Jaya grinned as she watched Emersyn open another set of double doors.

The bathroom was massive. A claw bath sat in one corner while in the other was a walk-in shower. Tucked away in the back right corner behind a half wall was the toilet. The last wall was filled with a long mirror that ran the expanse of the double sinks. The sinks were on top of the counters, with drawers underneath, and two matching stools with fluffy topped white cushions tucked underneath the counter bench. It was all decorated in soft grays and stark white with accents in a deeper gray. The wall with the walk-in shower was rough-hewn gray stone and the lighting came from muted pendants hanging in various places.

"Holy crap. Can I just move in here?" joked Jaya.

"There are far more important things to discuss than your living arrangements," Emersyn said seriously.

"And what would that be?"

"What are you going to wear?"

There was a knock on the door. "Lydia is here," Harvey announced before stepping aside to let the woman in. "Your platter will be up in a few minutes."

A skinny, long-tressed blonde with a fresh face, jeans and tank top followed behind Harvey. She carried a large make-up case and had a utility belt around her waist. "Heya, I'm Lydia." She spoke with the most Southern drawl Emersyn had ever heard. It was delightful.

"Hi, I'm Emersyn and this is Jaya." Emersyn turned to Jaya. "Lydia is here to make us even more beautiful for this evening. She comes highly recommended. Would you like to go first?"

"Mmm... thanks but I need to work out what I'm wearing first. Why don't you start and I'll do a fashion parade and you guys can help me pick out a dress for this evening?"

"Great plan," agreed Emersyn.

Chapter 18

Emersyn

The gold, backless dress was perfect. Emersyn adjusted the strap on her intricately laced high heels one last time and ran her fingers through her curled burgundy hair that hung over one shoulder, her bangs were swept to one side and the only jewelry she wore were a pair of thin, gold dangling earrings that almost grazed her shoulders, and a gold chain that had black diamonds spaced intermittently that ran down her back to join the deep V of her dress at the bottom. "You ready? You can help me greet everyone." Emersyn asked Jaya.

Jaya turned away from the full-length mirror in Emersyn's closest. "Lydia is a genius." Jaya's hair was piled seductively on the top of her head like she had just come from a romantic tryst with a handsome stranger. She wore a navy blue, satin jumpsuit with off the shoulder sleeves and a beaten silver chain around her waist. The heavy chain hung almost to her knees and was complimented by a thick silver choker, covered in diamonds that matched her nose piercing. The chocker had been a gift from Nicolai, and Emersyn had been surprised when she found herself suggesting to Jaya that she could borrow it.

The loud doorbell rang and both women giggled like school girls off to prom before they went to greet the first guests.

It didn't take long before the party was in full swing and Emersyn could move away from the meet and greet aspect of her hosting role and onto the more enjoyable mingling, eating, and drinking.

Matilda approached her. "Now I know why you declined my offer of help with planning the event. You have done an incredible job. Everything is just amazing." A waiter came by and offered them a mini lamb kofta, which they all took. "You used a different caterer to our usual one. I will have to get the number; I think they are better."

"I'm so pleased that you aren't offended. I love to plan these things, but never have the chance." Emersyn smiled broadly at Matilda.

"It would appear you are a woman of many talents. Not only did you come up with the original idea for the new Happy Girl campaign, you would make a very successful event planner."

"Oh, I didn't do anything that special. Arlo has to stop telling everyone that it was my doing. He did all the heavy lifting at the initial stages. I had no idea so much went into the planning even before you get the job."

"Where is Arlo? I haven't seen him all night." Matilda looked around.

"I'm not sure." Emersyn tried to look uninterested. It had been an uncomfortable moment when he had arrived as everyone was being greeted with hugs and kisses. Thankfully, Jaya had saved her by announcing that she couldn't possibly greet anymore people without a drink and dragged Arlo away with her to find a bar.

They were joined by a tall blond man with a broad, open smile and startling white teeth. He wore a bow tie that matched the purple fabric of Matilda's dress. "Hi." He smiled down at Emersyn.

"John, this is Emersyn. She is the host of this fabulous party." Matilda put her perfectly manicured hand on John's chest. "Emersyn, this is my husband, John. There were so many people when we got here that we snuck through the meet and greet bit."

She held out her hand for John to shake. "It is lovely to meet you."

Emersyn noted that the song had finished, but another song had not begun. "Can I have everyone's attention please?" Arlo spoke into the microphone.

"It looks like we found Arlo." Matilda smiled as everyone turned to the mini disco entrance.

"Can you all make your way into this very chic discotheque?" he asked. "And could Emersyn please come to the front with Mr. Tran?"

"Go and accept your accolades," urged Matilda. "You deserve them."

Emersyn snagged a glass of champagne as she made her way to where Arlo and Henry Tran stood. She hoped that Mr. Tran was one to keep his speeches short.

⸻ ◦○◦ ⸻

Emersyn stood with both her hands on the stone railing and took a minute to take in the surroundings from the view of the balcony. Now night had properly fallen, the lanterns that had been hung around the pool and the few that were floating in the pool were peaceful to look at. She might have to look at buying some. You could only see half of the pool as it was one of those designs where it bent around a corner to follow the shape of the house.

She breathed in deeply and let the chatter and music coming from the next room wash over her. The party appeared to be a success and now the speeches were over, people could either leave if they were so inclined or begin to relax. Arlo came to stand next to her and put his hand on the railing beside hers.

"Thank you," he spoke quietly. He didn't look at her and she kept her body facing out.

"For what?"

"For saving my ass and not gloating about it. I know I screwed up."

Emersyn wasn't truly listening to him. This was the closest they had been since they had been away and she was doing everything to not reach out those few inches to touch his hand. "Don't worry about it." Emersyn didn't want to have this conversation so she turned in the opposite direction to him to engage in conversation with anyone standing to the other side of her to only belatedly realize they were alone.

"I need to check on the party, excuse me." She made her excuse to leave and moved away from the balcony rail. Before she took more than a step, Arlo grabbed her forearm. Emersyn stared down at his hand as she registered his electrifying touch. Arlo grazed his hand down her arm, his fingertips lingered on hers as he reached her hand —they were barely connected but her body responded. Their fingers disconnected and the moment was lost. Emersyn went to leave again before she could no longer resist; her fingers itched to reach up and run her hand through his beautiful hair before grabbing it and pulling his soft lips down to hers.

Arlo moved to block her path but Emersyn moved around him.

"Why?" His voice was soft. None of the usual brashness.

"Why what?" She couldn't help herself. *Just walk away,* her brain screeched at her, but still she stood there, her back to him.

"Why do you always go?"

She stood there, caught. She felt the lightest touch of his fingertips begin at her wrists and travel up the back of her bare arms, coming to rest on her naked shoulders. *Is he trembling or is it me?* He now stood directly behind her and his breath was hot on her exposed neck. Both of them were breathing raggedly.

"Why?" he repeated the question, his voice barely above a whisper as if he was now afraid of the answer.

"Because I won't be a one-night stand and I could never survive anything more." Before he had the chance to respond she stepped forward, out of his touch. The spell was broken, and she could think clearly again. *Fuckk! That was close.*

Emersyn plastered a fake smile on her face and stepped through the open bi-fold doors and back into the crowd, grabbing a glass of champagne from the waiter and draining it, then putting it back on the tray as he moved past. She found Jaya in the lounge area, who promptly wanted to drag her out onto the dance floor. As they moved through the emptied dining room, where people mingled in small groups, Emersyn noted that Arlo was still standing on the balcony, his intense brown eyes followed her, giving nothing away. Emersyn shunted away her thoughts as she tried to reconcile Jaya's words that Arlo never slept with staff and the exceedingly clear invitation he had just extended.

As Emersyn walked into the makeshift nightclub, she tried to ignore the stab of jealousy as she watched Eva approach him and draw him away from the doorway and out of her sight. Jaya handed her another champagne that she downed as quickly as the previous one and they begin to dance. Several more of the people from the marketing department joined them on the dance floor as the smoke machine filled the room with bubble-gum scented smoke.

As the night wore on, Emersyn spent most of her time not knowing where Arlo was and pretending she didn't care, all the while acting like she was having a ball, in case he was watching.

Chapter 19

The pool water was refreshing as he slowly lowered his bare feet into it. Arlo rolled up his pant legs a few more times to make certain they didn't get wet, and put his shiny, leather shoes and socks behind him, out of the way. He slowly dragged his legs forwards and backward in the water, enjoying the music that came through the open doors on the balcony around the side of the house. It had taken him several false starts to find the entrance to the pool, and in the end he had given up and walked out the front door and followed the house around to his left until he came upon it. The pool was thinner in this section and only lit by tiny fairy lights in the surrounding shrubs; he assumed it was the lap pool section, with the larger pool—that you could see from the balcony—around the corner. He didn't want to be seen, so he had chosen to dangle his feet in this secluded part. He noted a large tree, he guessed an Angel Oak by the shape of the shadow on the opposite side of the pool. *That would make a great place to picnic,* he thought to himself.

It had been a long night and he hadn't enjoyed most of it. He felt like an impostor walking around accepting the congratulations on a job well done when he was the reason it could have all ended before it began. The fiasco that had occurred in LA had been kept between Henry Tran, the marketing team leaders, and Emersyn, which he would be forever grateful for. The speeches had been the worst: with everyone cheering while he watched Emersyn with her fake smile accept her minor role, when in fact without her the account would not have been obtained.

His attempt to once again get her to talk about what had happened had led to a revealing conversation that he was still trying to sort through. His mind wandered to the beautiful dress she wore tonight and the almost overwhelming want he had to slowly run his fingertips along her exposed spine, up into her curled hair, where he could gently take it in his fist and pull her head back to expose her throat, allowing him to trail kisses up to her full, burgundy painted lips. *What happened to your rule about not sleeping with staff?* he reminded himself. Emersyn would be a magnificent woman to bed, he admitted to himself, but he was more interested in seeking her approval and that surprised him.

Arlo was so caught up in his thoughts that he didn't notice he had company until it was too late.

"Do you mind if I join you?" Eva asked.

He looked up to find her standing there in a red, lace, half cup bra and matching G-string. "You lost your dress," he said. She had a well-toned body that would have made him hard in moments. Not today. All he thought about was the body encased in gold upstairs, having a great time while he was miserable.

She looked down in mock horror at her almost naked body. "Now, how did that happen?" Her black slip dress lay pooled next to her shoes and clutch, not far from where she stood. "It's awfully hot and stuffy in there. I was thinking of going for a swim." Her eyes were all wide-eyed innocence.

"Well, lucky for you there is a pool right here," laughed Arlo. He began to relax as Eva walked away, exposing her peached shaped bare bottom. This was his normal ground: where women flirted and he flirted and everyone knew the game. He watched with appreciation as Eva slowly walked into the pool, she lazily floated toward him, making sure that her hair and face never got wet.

"Would you care to join me?" She stopped in front of him and boldly placed her hands on his feet.

He leaned down, putting his hand in the water, and gently splashed her chest. "I'm good for the moment, but I appreciate the offer." He winked at her, picked up his drink, and took a large sip.

"You can't blame a girl for trying, and rumor has it you like secretaries." She grinned and ran her hands up his naked calf.

He spluttered the drink everywhere as he looked at her cheeky grin. "I would ask where you heard that, but I'm not sure I want to know." *Secretaries were definitely wonderful, but it would appear that I also like accountants...a lot,* he had to admit to himself.

Eva pushed herself away from Arlo and slowly swam around the pool. "This is truly divine. I had no idea that Emersyn was so rich. I mean her clothing and car are expensive, but this is next level. If I was this rich, I wouldn't bother to work."

"I don't think we should be gossiping about Emersyn. She has opened her home to us and that should never come with judgment." Arlo began to laugh as he ended his speech.

"What?"

"I just realized how much I sounded like my mother." He looked sheepish. "Sorry for the lecture."

"It's fine, you are right. I don't want people talking about me, so I shouldn't be talking about others." Eva looked serious in the dim light. "Well, I didn't think this through very well."

"You didn't? And here I was certain you knew exactly what you were doing."

Eva pouted. "There are no towels. How am I going to dry off?"

"Ah, I thought I saw a pool house from the balcony. Stay here and I'll have a look around."

"Stay here, he says," Eva muttered to herself. "Where else would I be going? Could you hurry up, I think the party is winding down."

<hr>

Emersyn

The last of the guests had gone and Emersyn now stood at the bottom of the gorgeous curved, marble staircase and wondered how she was going to get up to her bedroom. She had been a professional all night and no one would guess that she had drunk too much. Emersyn had instructed Harvey to tell all the staff to go home; the clean-up would happen tomorrow.

She held her champagne glass carefully in her hand as she slowly sank to the second step and looked down at the offending shoes that were stopping her from finding peace in bed. Her head swam more than a little from the number of French martinis and champagne she had drunk. Emersyn looked around forlornly and wondered if she could possibly crawl up the stairs in her tight dress without ruining it.

Arlo walked in through the front door and somewhere in the back of her mind registered that he had no shoes or socks on, and his suit pant legs were rolled up to just under his knees. His feet look damped. "You okay?" he asked.

"Everyone else has left. I thought you had gone too." She tried not to make it sound like an accusation.

"Without saying goodbye? I do have some manners." He scoffed.

She held up the glass as if to toast him. "Well, goodbye then." She downed half the glass and slid down the bottom steps and landed on the floor.

"Woah." He took the glass from her hand and placed it carefully on a nearby table. "Can you get up the stairs?"

"I can't figure out how to do that with these on," she admitted as she pointed to the offending killer heels.

He frowned as he looked at her shoes that wrapped around her ankles and up to her mid-calf. "I can see why you are having trouble."

"Here, let me do it," a chirpy voice came up behind him.

Eva appeared and Emersyn was only half aware that Eva appeared to be zipping up the side of her dress. Eva had no shoes on and her feet were also damp looking. "I have a similar pair, but not the real deal like these," she explained with a hint of envy as she quickly unknotted the ties and slid the shoes off. "There you go."

"Thank you." Emersyn thought she felt stable enough to try standing and pulled herself up to lean heavily on the balustrade. She stared at the two of them and didn't know what to say. She wanted Eva to leave and Arlo to carry her upstairs and lay her down on her bed and... she brought the thought to an abrupt halt.

"It was a wonderful party, Emersyn, thank you for having me." Eva smiled warmly. She turned to Arlo and put a hand on his arm. "Are you still good to give me a lift home?"

"Yes, grab our shoes and I'll meet you out by my car. It should be the only one left in the driveway."

A flash of pure jealously flooded Emersyn as she stood hanging onto the balustrade. She smiled benignly at Eva and kept her voice neutral. "I'm glad you enjoyed yourself. I'll see you at the office on Monday." She watched as the petite secretary walked out of the large entrance hall and through the open double front doors.

Emersyn turned to start her slow ascent up the stairs, gripping the railing without looking like she was. "Goodnight, Arlo. Thank you for coming, I hope you had a pleasant evening." She spoke airily as if she were dismissing him.

"Emersyn, please let me help you up the stairs."

Her anger flared. "I don't need anything from you."

He took a step back. "Where did that come from?"

"I am just being clear." She felt sick—too much champagne will do that. She needed him to leave so she could be drunk without his judgment. "Eva is waiting," she prompted. She resolutely kept her back to him, but she could feel his hesitation.

"You win. I will leave you alone. Good night, Emersyn." His words were gentle and kind.

She turned her head enough to watch him walk out the doors before Harvey closed and locked them. Emersyn slowly sank to her knees as soon as the doors were shut and closed her eyes only for them to spring back open as the room spun and it made her feel worse.

Harvey helped her to her feet and into her bedroom. He left her to get herself changed into an old t-shirt that was so worn the logo on the front was no longer recognizable. She climbed into her huge, comfortable bed and sat propped up, knowing that if she lie down, she would feel worse. Emersyn knew her body well enough to know that she needed fluids and to stay awake for at least an hour to allow the effects of the alcohol to wear off enough for her to sleep without being ill.

Harvey re-entered the bedroom with a tray laden with her Grandmother's favorite floral China tea set and a large glass of water. She took a few sips of the water as he prepared the tea.

"Are you planning on watching something, Miss Emersyn?" He picked up the remote that sat next to the television.

"Yes, I won't be able to sleep yet. Every time I close my eyes the room spins." She didn't add that she was haunted by Arlo's face. "Care to join me?"

Emersyn's bedroom was spacious with a large lounge over by the bay window. The TV could be swiveled enough to be watched from the lounge and the bed at the same time. It was not the first time Harvey would join Emersyn in some midnight viewing.

"What did you want to watch?" Harvey was a sucker for a Hallmark Murder Mystery romance, just like Emersyn.

"I recorded a couple of movies the other day that I am sure we will both like." Emersyn was already feeling better. She lay back and sipped her tea as the opening titles scrolled up. Harvey was dependable and safe—why couldn't all men be like that?

Chapter 20

Alo

The smell of coffee permeated the apartment as Arlo sat at the kitchen bench waiting for the machine to beep. He looked through his upcoming week's appointments that Mrs. Beaulieu had uploaded onto his calendar and was trying to figure out what he needed to work on first. As the coffee machine beeped, Eva walked in wearing Arlo's blue bath robe "Never took you for a robe type."

"We are all full of secrets." He smiled at her. He didn't want to tell her that he only had one for the women that slept over. For some reason, women loved a soft, fluffy gown to get into.

"Coffee?" she asked.

"Sure. White with one, thanks." All the things she needed to make a coffee were conveniently placed within easy reach of the machine. It stopped the need for his dates to go through his cupboards. She efficiently made him and herself a cup of steaming coffee and placed it near him on the counter.

Eva hummed softly to herself as she moved around the apartment. "Do you mind if I open the curtains? It looks like a gorgeous day out there."

He looked up from his laptop and smiled at her cheerfulness. "Sure." He closed his laptop and stretched his arms over his head, feeling his shoulders protest. *I could do with a workout.* His stomach growled, which caused Eva to giggle. "Want some breakfast? I make great waffles with berries," he asked.

"Sounds wonderful. Can I help?"

"Sure thing. You can wash and cut up the fruit."

"No problem."

As they worked together to create breakfast, Arlo asked Eva a few questions about her family and hobbies. She was happy to oblige and regaled him with some truly hilarious stories of her crazy half-brother's antics in their youth. Arlo couldn't help but compare Eva's easy, open chatter to Emersyn's cautious, always diverting conversations. She was so guarded, and he wondered if anyone had ever broken those shields? Or maybe they hurt her so badly that she had then put up her shields? Either way, it didn't matter; she had been clear about her want for him to stay away from her, even though he could have sworn that on the balcony she had given him a very clear idea that she wanted him but was too scared to follow through. He remembered the feel of her skin and burnt his hands on the waffle maker as he forgot where he was. "Shit," he swore as he sucked on his scorched thumb.

Eva came over to him and took his hand. "Let me see." She caressed his thumb before she lifted it and put it in her mouth, slowly sucking it in and running her tongue around it.

Arlo lost focus for a moment before he noticed the green light flashing on the waffle maker. "Waffles are ready," he announced and slowly withdrew his thumb from her mouth. "My thumb feels much better now, thanks." He winked at her before he finished assembling their breakfast.

"This is so freakin' yummy," Eva exclaimed as she dug into her food. "So, we still haven't solved the mystery of my missing keys."

"You must have left them at the party."

"Yes, my guess is they are somewhere near the pool. It's the only time I put down my purse."

"I guess you'll have to ring Emersyn and ask her to have a look around for you," Arlo said.

"Can't you do it for me?"

"What? Why?" Arlo almost choked on his waffle.

"Please? It's not like I have the head of accounting's cell number."

"I don't know."

"I thought you were on good terms after the success of the Happy Girl signing?" Eva looked puzzled.

"We are..." He left the sentence unfinished. He had no desire to talk to Eva about his tangle of emotions concerning Emersyn. "Why don't I give you the number and you can ring?"

Eva just stared at him, a slow smile spreading across her face. "Sooo," she dragged out the word. "You won't just ring Emersyn and ask her to search for my keys near the pool because..." She left the rest unsaid.

"Fine," he growled and stood to grab his phone. Quickly he sent a text to Jaya, not wanting to involve his PA, Mrs. Beaulieu, asking her to contact Emersyn and see if they could possibly try to find Eva's keys and that he believed they were somewhere near the pool. And if the keys were found, did she want him to pick them up. Or, if they were dropped off, could it be at his place and gave her the address.

He waited for some jibe from Jaya about why Eva was at his place, but it never came.

⚬

Emersyn

Bright sunlight shone through the cracks of the heavy curtains that covered Emersyn's large bedroom windows, letting her know just how late she had slept. Her room had become hot and stuffy and her head pounded. Bitter thoughts swam to the surface as she lie there and she didn't like the picture they were painting. *Why did Arlo and Eva have no shoes on? Was Eva doing up her zip? Why hadn't she seen either of them the last hour of the party as the crowd thinned and she wished everyone a goodnight?* There were too many questions to think of with a foggy head. Emersyn reached over and pressed the buzzer that was on her bedside table.

As she continued to lie there, she began to register the noises coming up from downstairs. The cleaning crew had probably arrived and started cleaning so they could put her furniture back. She lie there a few moments longer and decided that while she waited for Harvey to bring her morning tea, she needed a shower and to brush her teeth. Her mouth was fuzzy, she still had her make-up on, and she hoped that her head would clear once she put it under the water.

A loud groan left her as she threw back the blanket and swung her feet to the floor. It didn't take long for her to shower and change into a pair of worn, jean shorts and a spearmint green mid-drift t-shirt. She pulled her hair up into a messy ponytail and sat down on the window seat that overlooked a part view of the garden and a partial view of the driveway. Harvey had placed the tea tray on the bay window seat and she made herself a cup of hot English breakfast tea. Emersyn sipped on the tea as she watched the comings and goings of the clean-up crew as they dismantled the bars and nightclub and loaded it back onto trucks for the next event.

"Bugger." Suddenly she remembered she wanted to keep the lanterns that had been hanging in the pool area and put down her tea and went in search of flip flops at the bottom of her closest. "I hope they haven't taken them yet," she spoke to no one.

Her phone pinged as she went to put it in her pocket, so she took it back out to discover a text from Jaya.

J: Hey Hun, great night last night. Thanks again for having Lydia make me even more awesome. When you get a chance, can you please check around the pool area? Eva can't find her keys and thinks they may have ended up there. xx

E: Hey Luv, you are awesome without any help from Lydia. I'll look around the pool for the keys. Not sure why they would be around there??? Seems odd. xox

J: Very odd. Even odder that Arlo sent me a message to ask you. He said if you find them, he can come and get them, or could you get them couriered to him at his place? xx

E: His place? Arlo asked you? You know what...I don't want to know. I'll check now and get back to you. xox

Emersyn looked at the texts and her heart sank as she put all the images from last night together with the text about missing keys by the pool. She didn't like where it all led. Eva and Arlo had obviously been out by the pool, which explained the lack of shoes and dress, and Arlo texting this morning about missing keys and getting them to his place, which could only mean that Eva had spent the night.

As she walked down the stairs, she was greeted by several workmen in overalls and the sound of vacuuming. Emersyn went out the front door and around the side of the house rather than through the downstairs family area that opened up onto the pool section as it was quicker and less crowded.

The crushed rock from the driveway crunched under her feet as she stomped around the side of the house and toward the pool. *Why are you so upset?* she asked herself as she came to the beginning of the lap pool area. Emersyn was about to walk by when she noticed a towel draped over a chair on the opposite side of the pool. How did that get there? It was a striped white and yellow towel that belonged in the pool house. Backtracking. Emersyn went around to the white wrought iron table and chairs and felt a lump under her shoe. She took a step back to find a set of keys with a pink, sparkly heart twinkling in the sun. For some reason, her heart plummeted; even though she had been sure they had been out here, the towel and keys were further proof. Her mind shunned the idea of what exactly had occurred in her pool.

"Miss Emersyn." Harvey brought her back to the moment. He looked concerned, which was unusual.

Ah, what now? she wondered. "Hi Harvey. I found these keys, they belong to one of the secretaries. I'll give you an address that they need to be couriered to immediately." She bent down and scooped up the keys and grabbed the towel. "I think one of our guests had a dip last night." She handed the towel to him as well.

"Miss Emersyn," Harvey spoke softly. "I'm not sure why but Samantha Hufferton is here with the child. And she is demanding to see you."

Emersyn scowled at the air in front of her until she registered that she was staring at the huge Angel Oak tree in the distance that had been her mother's favorite place to picnic. What she wouldn't give to be a little girl again without any of the concerns and scars she carried with her now.

"I can tell her you are unavailable."

"No, let's get this over with." As she walked back to the front door, she texted Jaya.

E: Hey, found the keys. Send me the address and I will have them sent to him. Xox

J: K. Lunch tomorrow?" xx

E: I have meetings all day. I'll let you know. xox

Jaya sent the address and Emersyn forwarded it to Harvey to deal with while she took a deep steadying breath before she entered her home to face Samantha Hufferton.

Chapter 21

Emersyn

Samantha Hufferton was a socialite that had been disowned by her rich, God-fearing family when they had discovered that she was with child to another woman's husband. That woman had been Emersyn Cole and it had been the final nail in the proverbial coffin to her marriage to Nicolai Webb. Gritting her teeth, Emersyn walked through the double front doors and found Samantha and her little girl standing in the center of the foyer, amongst the bustling workmen. It astounded Emersyn that Samantha couldn't see she was directly in the path of furniture being moved, but then this woman had been raised to put her own interests and wellbeing above all others.

"Why didn't you respond to my email?" Samantha demanded as soon as she spotted Emersyn.

"Hello, Samantha. How are you?" Emersyn chose to ignore the question. "What a beautiful little girl you have. What is her name?"

The closer Emersyn got to the child, tiny shards of her heart tore off. The chubby-faced little girl was a true mix of her parents. She had Nicolai's nose, full mouth, and chin, combined with her mother's pale blue eyes and peaches and cream complexion. Though Samantha looked a lot less peaches and cream and more pale custard with browning bananas under her eyes at the moment.

"Sahara," answered Samantha.

"A powerful name. I hope she lives up to it." Emersyn saw Harvey talking to one of the garden staff who had come in to help clean up. He handed over Eva's keys and a slip of paper, which she assumed was Arlo's address. She got his attention and he walked over. "Is the kitchen done yet?"

"Yes, Miss Emersyn."

"Thank you. That's where we shall be." Emersyn turned back to Samantha. "Would you and Sahara like to follow me? We need to talk somewhere a little more private. The world doesn't need to know our business."

Samantha nodded, scooped up Sahara, and followed Emersyn through the house to the sun-filled kitchen. An old, round oak table sat in a breakfast nook that was filled with hanging fern plants, giving the area a cool feel even with the sun coming in. "Would you like a drink? I think we have fresh lemonade."

"No, thank you, but Sahara will have milk, if she can."

"I think I have cookies or would you prefer her to have fruit?" Emersyn was aware that she was stalling.

"She can have a cookie, thank you."

The silence built as Emersyn moved around the kitchen, getting Sahara's food and pouring herself a glass of lemonade. Finally, she sat opposite the pair and waited for Samantha to tell her why she had come.

"You need to give Nicki back his money, so he can pay for Sahara."

Emersyn almost laughed at the sheer audacity of the woman. Nicolai was many things, but he had never been one to shirk his responsibilities. "He is not paying you child support?" She deliberately added a little shock to her voice.

"Well, yes, he is," she admitted. "But it is not enough. I need more." Her voice was whinny.

Emersyn was certain that some men found that whinny voice cute, but Emersyn just found it annoying. "You need to go through a lawyer if you want Nicolai to pay you more. Why would you think this has anything to do with me?"

Sahara finished her cookie and now began to fidget. It looked like Samantha had not come prepared with anything to entertain her daughter. Finally, she took out her phone, flicked a few things, and handed the phone to the little girl. Emersyn could hear the faint sounds of the beginning of a Disney movie.

"Nicki says you took most of his money and that's why he can't pay me more."

"I didn't take any of his money. I took what was mine and left."

Samantha looked pointedly around the large kitchen and would have raised an eyebrow if she could. "You seriously expect me to believe that you didn't take any of his money?"

Emersyn leaned forward and spoke quietly. She was getting frustrated but didn't want to raise her voice in front of Sahara. "Do I look like I need the man's money?"

"You only have this house because of the money you took," countered Samantha.

"Wrong. This is my father's house."

"What about the fast car and designer clothes?"

Emersyn sighed. "You do know what a job is, right? I pay my way."

"I've never had a job. I never needed one. Daddy always paid my bills. I had no idea how much things cost," Samantha admitted. "The money Nicki gives me doesn't even cover my costs."

"It's not supposed to cover your costs, it is supposed to take care of your child's needs. You come second."

"Then how am I supposed to take care of me?"

Emersyn barely refrained from reaching over and shaking the young socialite. "That job that I mentioned? You need to get one." She stopped and looked at the woman who had helped to ruin her marriage and then at Sahara, who had no fault in the mess, but who would end up paying the price. "If you need a job, I may be able to help you. I still have friends at my old job, I'm sure they could find something for you."

"A job? Me?"

"Sure, you should work. It gives you the freedom to not rely on anyone and it shows Sahara that a woman can stand on her own."

Samantha ran her fake, perfectly manicured nails through her platinum blonde hair, that held no trace of regrowth—it was obvious where the child support was going. "I don't think a job is the answer to my problems. I think you are lying about where the money came from and should give it back to Nicki." The whinny tone increased as the volume did.

"Be reasonable. Why would I have any need to lie to you?" Emersyn tried to keep calm but was nearing the end of her patience with the woman.

"You know Nicki said you were too driven to succeed and were overly demanding in your want for everything to be perfect. That's why he picked me. I am fun and easy going and spontaneous." Samantha's tone had become nasty.

"And yet here we are, both alone. If he wanted you, why aren't you still together?" Emersyn dragged in a breath through her gritted teeth. "I think it's best if you leave. We have nothing further to discuss. My advice to you is to do what the rest of the women of the world do. Get a job and support your child."

"I'm not going anywhere until I get what I came for." Samantha stood up, her chair falling backward onto the dark tiled floor.

The noise brought Harvey into the room. "Can I help with something, Miss Emersyn?"

"Yes. Samantha and Sahara were just leaving, please show them out."

Samantha remained stationary for a few minutes longer before she gathered her bag and picked up Sahara. "Fine, I'll go." She sneered at Emersyn as she moved. "But this isn't over."

Emersyn shook her head. "If you want money you need to beg your parents for forgiveness or get a lawyer to ask Nicolai for money, but keep me out of it." The words she wanted to put at the end of the sentence remained unsaid for the sake of the child.

As soon as they left the kitchen, Emersyn slumped down in her chair. Tears slowly crept down her cheeks as what Samantha had said registered. "I can be fun, easy going, and spontaneous," she whispered into the air. "I just have to be in a safe space." That last statement made her straighten her shoulders and wipe her hand over her face as she came to the realization that Nicolai had never made her feel safe enough to drop the shields she had built as a teenager to cope with a dead mother and an absent father.

Chapter 22

Arlo

It had been several weeks since the party, and Arlo continued to war with his heart over what he felt about Emersyn. He was either denying her existence by hiding from her or making excuses to go up to the floor her office was on just to walk by in the off chance of seeing her. It was all new territory for him, and he didn't like it at all. Arlo had never longed for a woman like this. She was complicated and intense and completely infuriating. Her expectations were high of those she worked with and he assumed those in her personal life. The more he had gone over their conversation on the balcony at the work party, the more he didn't understand what had happened. He knew when a woman wanted him and it was clear that night that she desired him as much as he desired her. How did it end up going so wrong, with her telling him to leave her alone? He could see it in her green eyes that she was caught by her feelings and scared, but what she was scared of was something he didn't comprehend.

Arlo looked at the pile of files on his desk that needed to go back up to the same floor the accounting staff was on. *Mrs. Beaulieu is getting older, maybe I should just take them up to help out?* he reasoned with himself. Quickly, he gathered them up and left his office to find Mrs. Beaulieu sitting at her desk looking at him expectantly. "Do you need me to file those?" she asked.

"Ah, they need to go upstairs."

"I could do with stretching my legs." She held out her hand.

Arlo hesitated. How did he tell his mature aged PA that he was making up excuses to go see a girl?

"Is there a problem, Mr. Medina?"

It didn't matter how many times he had requested she call him Arlo, Mrs. Beaulieu refused. "No, no. I was thinking of heading to lunch early and thought I'd just drop them off. Save you a bit of time."

Mrs. Beaulieu looked over the top of her thick-framed, black glasses and shook her head slightly, causing her silver, bobbed hair to gently sway. They stared at each other for a few more moments before Arlo finally gave up and handed over the files. He went to walk back into his office when Mrs. Beaulieu spoke. "I thought you were heading out for an early lunch?"

"Oh, yeah." Arlo did an about face and headed out the door. He got to the end of the corridor and paused; he wasn't hungry he just wanted an excuse, now it had backfired.

"Hey, Arlo? Are you going to lunch?" Eva walked up beside him.

"Yes, taking an early one today. Got a lot to get ready this afternoon for tomorrow's meeting." He pushed the elevator button. *I'll just grab a coffee,* he told himself.

"Can I join you? I wanted to ask a few questions about different departments and career advancement." Eva looked hopeful.

"Sure, but my first piece of advice would be to stay as the secretary of our department for a year to get a feel for what area interests you the most."

The elevator doors slid open and they both got in. "Great. Thanks for this."

As they traveled down the floors, Arlo told her an amusing story about his early days at the agency. He grinned as Eva gripped his forearm while she bent over laughing. The doors slid open to the foyer and the grin slipped from Arlo's face as he looked up to find startled, emerald eyes looking at them.

"Emersyn, how are you?" Eva asked as they stepped out of the elevator and she stepped in.

"I'm great. And you?" Emersyn didn't look at Arlo, she just pushed the floor button.

"Fabulous," Eva announced as the doors closed. "My goodness, she is a beautiful woman. I would kill for those eyes and lips." She turned to look at Arlo. "Don't you think?"

Arlo was having trouble breathing. He was still trying to understand the look on Emersyn's face. When the door had opened his instinct had been to snatch his arm away from Eva, which would have been ridiculous as he was doing nothing wrong. "Yes, Emersyn is very pretty." He needed to change the subject. "Did you want to get Japanese? There is a great place around the corner."

"Yum. Let's go."

<hr>

"You know what you are?" Jaya said as she continued to flip through the folder Arlo had just handed to her.

"Mmm, I'm a great boss who is giving you a great opportunity to take the lead in this and continue to grow under my marvellous tutelage," Arlo said lightly.

"Very funny."

"Thank you."

Jaya looked up from the folder and straight at Arlo. "You, my wonderful boss, are a coward."

"How's that?" He regretted asking it the moment it came out. He knew that he had now opened himself up to, what Jaya would call, constructive criticism.

"Because you may be pretending to yourself that you are doing me this huge favor, but we both know you don't want to go to the monthly review because you can't face Emersyn." She went back to perusing the folder. "I just wish one of you would be honest with yourself, if not each other."

"I have no idea what you are talking about," Arlo protested.

"Really? You are avoiding her by making me take more meetings than ever before."

"You need to learn these things. What happens if I choose to take a long holiday?" he countered.

Jaya plunged on without comment. "And she is avoiding you, by not coming here to ever collect me for lunch. Now I just get a text to meet her downstairs." Her brown eyes narrowed as she studied him. "Did something happen at the party? It's like the animosity from her has grown since then. I knew she was mad at what happened in LA, but on her behalf, she appears to be angrier."

Arlo let out his breath and looked at Jaya, bewildered. "I really don't know what happened."

Chapter 23

Arlo

Arlo's phone rang, so he grabbed it, and for one irrational moment hoped that it was Emersyn needing him for some reason. He was disappointed to see Sarah's name appear on the screen. Sarah was a florist he had been dating on and off for a few months, but she was becoming needier the more often they caught up. Arlo had been clear as to what he wanted, but she had chosen to ignore him and make it into more in her head. He had attempted to end it several weeks prior when he had finished his relationships with Felicity and Milly, but Sarah just kept holding on. It was time to be very clear, but he didn't want to hurt her.

"Hey, Sarah," he answered the phone. Fifteen minutes later and he was finally confident that Sarah understood that they would no longer be seeing each other in any capacity.

It was late Saturday afternoon, and for the third week in a row Arlo had no plans for the evening. He found it freeing and didn't know why. He wondered what Emersyn was doing at the moment and told himself to stop it. Arlo had decided to do no work today and just take time for himself. There was always talk about women needing their 'me time.' Why weren't men encouraged to take it? He had been to the gym, then off to the barbers before finishing off his 'me time' with a wonderful massage. Making himself another coffee, he decided to call his parents. He knew his mother would be home but wasn't confident about his dad. His dad worked late on Saturday afternoons when the business was busy.

Arlo pressed the Facetime call button and waited patiently for his mother to figure out what was happening and how to answer it. Finally, her pretty face filled the screen and she smiled, thrilled to see him. "Hey, Mom," Arlo said.

"My baby boy, how are you?" she asked but didn't give him time to reply. "Is everything okay? You usually are busy getting ready to go out on a Saturday night."

Arlo laughed. He could have predicted exactly the words that she had just uttered. "Mom, I'm fine. I'm just taking some time out from dating."

Her hazel eyes narrowed as if she could see him better through the screen that way. "Why are you taking time out from dating?" She held her hand up. "Not that I am complaining. All those women make my head spin."

"I just wasn't feeling like it."

"Hang on, your papa has just walked in." Her face disappeared from the screen, but she could be heard yelling. "Luis, Arlo is on the screen, hurry up!"

"Just need to wash my hands and I'll be right there."

Tracy's face appeared back on the screen. "He's on his way. How is work? Anything exciting coming up?"

They chatted for a few minutes about work and the current campaigns he was working on. Arlo carried the laptop into the kitchen and placed it on the bench while he went about making his dinner.

"Arlo, how are you?" asked Luis as he put his face too close to the screen.

"Hey, Papa, take a step back. I can't see Mom."

"Oops, sorry. I always do that."

Tracy laughed and squeezed her husband's arm as she came back into view. He winked at her and joined in her laughter.

It was the first time Arlo had noticed his parents' warmth towards each other. They were never particularly demonstrative when he was growing up. They never kissed or held hands and his mother would forever complain that Luis wasn't listening to her—he had assumed they were bored with each other. Could he have been wrong about their relationship this whole time? Did you need to have public affection to have deep love? Had he been searching for the wrong thing?

"Do you have a late date tonight?" asked his father.

"No, I haven't been dating much lately. I just needed a break. They are always great girls, but..." He didn't know how to finish the sentence.

Luis and Tracy sat down on the couch and propped him up on the coffee table. "How's Santana?" Arlo asked.

"You should ring your sister. She would love to hear from you."

"I might do that after I hang up with you guys."

"Papa, tell me about the store." Arlo switched to Spanish.

Luis launched into a detailed story of the latest drama of the teenage staff that helped him and the afternoon crept into the night without Arlo noticing.

———◈———

Emersyn

"Cheers."

"Cheers." Jaya clinked her glass against Emersyn's. "To fabulous friends."

It was late Saturday afternoon and they were several drinks into their get together. "To day drinking."

Music played loudly and left-over gourmet pizza lie abandoned on the table as the two women sat on the balcony and watched the sun slowly move toward the horizon. It had been a perfect Fall day, and they had spent it at the spa and hair salon in the morning, picking up a pizza on the way home, and then spending the remainder of the afternoon taking turns to pick their favorite songs from the music streaming app and having Harvey mix them cocktails. They had thought it quite hysterical when they had asked Harvey to make them a Harvey Wallbanger.

It was wonderful for Emersyn to relax and enjoy time being the real person she was, rather than the woman who was always in control. Jaya had proven to be a true friend over the months since Emersyn had started at Chalmers and Tran, and she was slowly letting her guard down in response to that. She hadn't let anyone in since she had walked out on Nicolai and her old life. Several friends had attempted to contact her early on in the separation, but every time she spoke to someone, she found out that they had known what was happening behind her back and had chosen to keep his secret and make her look stupid for not knowing what was happening until Samantha had spelled it out. She pushed the thoughts away. It is done now. But was it done? Did she not keep Arlo at a distance because she was terrified of trusting, and he had shown that when it came to women, he was a player?

"Do you think Arlo is sleeping with Eva?" she blurted out to Jaya.

Jaya coughed as she tried to swallow her drink. "Is that what has been bothering you?"

"What do you mean?"

"You two are driving me crazy with your games."

"I'm not playing any games," insisted Emersyn. "Arlo's the one who is good at games."

"Maybe 'games' was the wrong word." Jaya took a long drink, ignoring the glare she received from her friend.

"You avoid him, he avoids you. You make it so you just happen to be at the right place so you can torture yourself and watch as he walks by and he finds excuses to go up to your level just to see if you are in your office. Yet, neither of you will admit anything and just continue to insist that I am crazy."

"You didn't answer my question."

"Oh, didn't I?" Jaya grinned and took another sip. "Annoying, isn't it?"

Emersyn laughed and finished her drink. Pouring out the remainder of the current cocktail into their now empty glasses from a heavy glass ewer that Harvey had left for them as he went in search of Blue Curacao because Jaya was adamant that Emersyn would love a 'Fruit Tingle.' Emersyn grabbed a piece of the now cold pizza and began to chew on it, as she attempted to avoid asking the question again.

Jaya took the last slice and sat happily munching on it. Pretending that she didn't know exactly what she was doing.

It had now come down to a test of wills. The music stopped and Emersyn wiped her hands on her wrap dress before picking up her phone to skim through and find another song. She let the first few bars of the song play before she resumed eating her pizza.

"Fine." Jaya gave in. "I don't know if they are sleeping together. I don't think so though, as he has made no mention of moving her on. Matter of fact, last week he was talking about how she had expressed interest in finding her niche and his advice had been to stay on as secretary for a year so she could get a feel for what we do over small and large accounts." Jaya finished her pizza and wiped her hands on Emersyn's dress, which made Emersyn shout with laughter.

As they settled back into their chairs and watched the sun-kissed horizon Jaya asked, "Why do you ask if they are?"

"After the party, I couldn't get up the stairs, I couldn't undo my stupid shoes. Arlo and Eva came in and rescued me, but at the time I was too drunk to register much. It wasn't until the next morning and the whole missing keys text that I realized that they both had no shoes on and Eva had been zipping up her dress when they had come to say goodbye and found me at the bottom of the stairs."

"And then she was at his place when the keys were discovered missing," added Jaya.

Emersyn nodded. "I also saw them in the lift the other day. She was hanging onto his arm, very intimately, and they were laughing."

"That does put a different spin on things," admitted Jaya.

Harvey coughed slightly to announce his return. "I found the Blue Curacao, Miss Jaya. Would you care to show me how to make a Fruit Tingle?"

Jaya jumped up. "Absolutely."

The music faded and before there was a chance to put another song on, Emersyn's phone pinged with a notification. She didn't like to check her phone when she was with people, she found it rude, but Jaya was busy with Harvey. The text was from Henry Tran.

H: Sorry to bother you on a Saturday, but Arthur Chalmers is flying in next week and would like to meet you. We thought you might like to join us for dinner one night?

E: Hi, Mr. Tran. Dinner to meet Mr. Chalmers sounds great. I am free any night, just let me know which one suits you.

HT: Thank you, Emersyn. I'll get back to you regarding a date. We would appreciate it if you kept the dinner quiet. Enjoy the rest of your weekend.

E: Of course. You too.

Thoughts of the text went out of her head as Jaya called out, "Emersyn, it's time to go old school. Put on something that I can sing badly to."

"Sing, really?" Emersyn fake grimaced.

Emersyn lie back in the claw foot bathtub that dominated her gorgeous bathroom. Softer music now filled the air and she was only a little buzzed from the multitude of cocktails that had been ingested. Jaya had left about half an hour ago, and Emersyn had tried to help Harvey clean up until she had dropped a glass and had to be carried out of the room because she had no shoes on. He had suggested a nice long, bubble bath and said that he would be up with some tea and maybe they could watch a movie later. Emersyn had gladly agreed and now she floated in the bubbles, trying to keep her wandering mind at bay.

She worried about Samantha and if she had seen the last of her, which led her to start thinking about Nicolai and the shattered heart she had had to repair when all his secrets were revealed. It had taken months for her to gather up the shards and slowly put them back together, in some semblance of what her heart looked like. Would it ever be as trusting and able to love in the same capacity? She just didn't know, and more importantly, she didn't want to find out.

Being alone was enjoyable most of the time. She had Jaya and she still kept in contact with a few college friends. And there was, of course, Harvey. The man was a saint and had been the rock she needed while she healed.

As Emersyn grabbed the soap and began to wash herself, her thoughts turned to an olive-skinned, handsome face, with short, wavy, dark brown hair and deep brown eyes. Her hand slid over her shoulder, down to her breast and her nipple hardened with the sensation. Her hand slid over her stomach and hovered between her thighs for several long moments. It had been a long time since Emersyn had thought about sex in any capacity, and as her fingers slowly began to move, she realized how much she missed the pure, joyous sensations of it.

Chapter 24

Emersyn

The veal was incredible and the wine had been amazing. Emersyn was full but the lemon meringue pie that had just been carried past their table had caught her attention. Maybe she could grab one at the end of the evening and take it home to share with Harvey?

Arthur Chalmers and Henry Tran had been wonderful hosts for the entire meal. Making her feel welcome and heaping her with praise on the job she was doing. They had both insisted she call them by their first names. Arthur was a handsome man closing in on retirement age, but he had a full head of silver hair and took great care of himself, as he didn't have the middle-age spread many men got.

"Would you excuse me, please?" Henry asked as he stood and placed his napkin down.

"Of course. Shall I start without you?" Arthur asked.

"Sure, I won't be long."

Emersyn smiled as Henry left and Arthur turned to face her. "Emersyn, Henry can't speak highly enough of you and I wanted to add my personal congratulations on the Happy Girl account."

"Happy Girl was very much a team effort. Arlo has a gift for knowing what the clients want." Emersyn didn't feel comfortable taking the credit for Arlo's work.

"The company figures, here in Austin, have increased an impressive amount since you took the reins."

She blushed at the compliment. "Thank you. I have made a few people unhappy."

"They are usually the ones that don't work hard enough," Arthur observed. "Emersyn, even though you have only been with us for a little over five months, we can see how much of an asset you have become and would like to offer you the role of head of accounts at the new office we are planning on opening in LA." Arthur smiled warmly at her. "What do you think?"

Their conversation was interrupted by a loud crash as a waiter dropped his tray. Everyone in the dining room of Romanos looked to see what had happened. Emersyn was shocked to see Arlo bending down, with a gorgeous woman in a red dress next to him, helping clean up the plates that had fallen. The Maître De was trying to get them both to stand up, insisting that they didn't have to help. Arlo looked up and stared at Emersyn, then quickly looked down again when he found her looking at him. A waiter stood to one side, holding several brown bags. He handed one to Arlo and the other to the woman and they quickly left together.

"What was that all about?" asked Henry as he returned to the table.

"I was just offering Emersyn the position in LA when one of the waiters got a bit clumsy and dropped a tray."

Henry turned to Emersyn. "What do you think? Are you open to the idea of moving already? I know you have only been here a short time, and relocating is a pain. We would be happy to foot the bill for all your costs and find you a place to live."

"To be honest, I am shocked by the offer. I feel like I only just found my feet here. Will you be offering anyone else in this office the chance to move?" Emersyn was hoping that if she chose to take the job, she would know at least a few people.

"We were looking at offering the senior role to Arlo, but we don't think it's a good idea if he goes to LA at the moment," Henry said.

Arthur looked serious. "No, we need that to be out of people's memories a little longer and he needs to learn his lesson."

They both looked at her. Emersyn was incredulous that they thought she could make this decision so lightly that she would accept here and now. "I am going to need some time to think things over. Could I give you my answer on Monday?"

"That seems reasonable," answered Arthur.

"Could I interest you in another wine, Emersyn?" Henry asked.

"No, thank you, I am driving." Another waiter walked by with a delicious looking piece of lemon meringue pie. "Could I have a pot of tea and one of those." She pointed at the dessert. "If that is okay?"

"That sounds like a grand idea. I'll have one too," said Arthur.

Henry ordered their desserts and drinks before turning back to Emersyn. "We would like your opinion on a few people we were thinking of recruiting to the LA office from different departments. There will be about ten from the Austin office and ten from the New York office."

"Who will be the CEO?" Emersyn asked.

"Henry's daughter and son will step in here and Henry will take LA. They don't have the experience individually to run here, but together and with Arlo's expertise they should be fine," Arthur explained. "You will also need to let us know if you take the job, who you think would be capable of doing your role."

The waiter brought out the dessert and Emersyn took her first bite. It was divine. The lemon curd was tart and the meringue fluffy, with that slightly crisp top making the combination heaven.

Emersyn looked at the two men. "Okay, hit me with the first name. Who do you have in mind?"

They spent the remainder of the evening going over people that the men had suggested may be willing to move and were capable of stepping up and leading in such a cutthroat city. Emersyn didn't think about Arlo and the mystery girl in the red dress until she was on her way home. For some bizarre reason, even though he was out on another date, she was relieved that he wasn't with Eva.

◆

Arlo

It's a good sign, he told himself as he found a car park right out the front of the restaurant on a Friday night. He had worked late and didn't feel like dinner, but had had a craving for Romanos lemon meringue pie. Since he had stopped dating, he hadn't needed to keep his fridge stocked with a slice of yummy dessert to entice his ladies back to his place. Dessert was much classier than coffee, he had always thought.

Arlo noted that the dining room was packed tonight. As he walked up to the desk to order, he took a seat next to an elderly couple who sat quietly in companionable silence. Normally he would have dragged his phone out to look busy, but this time he just sat and looked around. A beautiful woman in a tight red dress smiled at him from the other side of the foyer. He returned the smile, but instead of attempting to engage her in flirting, he simply moved his eyes onto the gentlemen sitting beside her.

It didn't take long for his name and another name to be called as a waiter walked out of a swinging door carrying brown paper bags. Arlo stood, as did the woman in the red dress, and they moved toward the waiter at the same time. He had been raised correctly and had taken a step to the side, ending up in the entrance of the dining room, to allow her to collect her take-away first.

His heart felt like it had moved up into his throat before plummeting into his stomach as he saw Emersyn having dinner with a very handsome, distinguished looking gentlemen. She looked wonderful. Her hair was gleaming brightly in the restaurant's fancy lighting and she wore an off one shoulder, emerald green dress, that he knew would perfectly match her eyes. He panicked and stepped back, directly into the path of a waiter and the heavily laden tray he was carrying.

As the tray crashed to the ground, the lady in the red dress joined him in helping to pick up the mess he had created. The maître de appeared horrified that they were cleaning up and kept asking them to stop. Arlo took the risk and glanced up only to find Emersyn staring at him, so he quickly returned to gathering plates and food. The man she was with was taking no notice of what was happening.

"Sir, Ma'am, please stand up. That is not necessary," the maître de spoke firmly.

"Okay, sorry. Just trying to help." They both spoke as they stood.

The waiter handed them each a paper bag.

Arlo didn't risk another glance at Emersyn as he took his bag and walked out, holding the door open for the woman in red.

"Thank you," she said and again smiled at him in a way he knew meant that she would be happy to stop and chat.

"You're welcome. Have a good night." He smiled and got into his car. He just wanted to get as far away from Romanos as he could.

Arlo turned the stereo on and asked his phone to play his current favorite song. He played it loud in an attempt to drown out the thoughts that wanted to surface. It didn't help. *Who was the guy she was with? I thought she wasn't dating,* his inner voice told him. *Maybe she just doesn't want to date you.*

By the time he got home he had played so many scenarios over in his head, he was beginning to develop a headache. "Why is it bothering you so much?" he asked the emptiness of his kitchen as he tore open the paper bag and grabbed a fork.

He had no answer or at least one he was comfortable with. To fill the silence, he turned on the TV and flicked through till he found some basketball to watch. He spread out on the couch and spent the next hour pretending to watch the TV while slowly eating his way through his dessert.

Finally, he couldn't stand it any longer and picked up his phone, and scrolled through his contacts until he found Emersyn's number. *You're an idiot. She's probably still out on her date. Put the phone down.* He needed a distraction. He noted a contact he had been meaning to catch up with for a while and decided that now was as good a time as any to find out if they were available. He flicked them a text.

A: Hey, how you doing? Sorry I haven't been in touch for a while, things have been crazy at work. I know it's a long shot, but you free for a drink tonight?

R: Great to hear from you. Give me an hour and I will meet you at the usual?

A: Yeah, great. See you there.

Arlo hauled himself off the couch and into the shower. It didn't take him long to get ready. He tidied up the left-over lemon meringue and flicked off the TV; grabbing his keys and jacket he headed out the door to hopefully a night where he would completely forget the name Emersyn Cole.

Chapter 25

Emersyn

*H*e pushed her up against the wall and pressed his lips to hers, giving her no time to think, no time to hesitate. She responded by pressing herself against him. Every inch of her wanted him to touch her. One of his hands moved up from her waist, grazing the side of her breast and continuing onto the base of her neck, where he wrapped her hair in his fist. She groaned and pushed her groin against his. Her hand slid down his back and came to rest on his ass, gripping him to keep him against her, she slowly rotated her hips. Arlo halted the kiss and stared at her, not breaking the look while his hands found the zip that ran down the back of her dress. It was as if he were waiting for her to stop him. She didn't want to stop him, she realized. Slowly the zip lowered.

No! Wake up, she told herself. Emersyn sat up in bed and fought for her head to clear and focus on the fact that she was alone. *Ughh, this is getting ridiculous.* This was the third night this week she had dreamt of Arlo. *I should work out more. You always sleep better after you run*, she told herself. May as well start now. She had a great deal to consider after the unexpected job offer at dinner last night and pounding through a run on the treadmill might help her come to a decision.

As she threw on her workout gear, Harvey knocked on her bedroom door. "Hang on," she called. After finishing getting dressed, she opened the door to Harvey. "Good morning, Harvey."

"Good morning, Miss Emersyn. Would you be wanting breakfast?"

"I'm going to work out first and then an egg white omelet would be great," she told him as she walked out of her room and headed toward the fully equipped gym that took up half of the pool house and overlooked the gardens. It had huge sliding windows that she opened to let in the fresh Fall air and the quiet sounds of birds twittering.

For once it felt good to sweat. Emersyn slowed down the speed of the treadmill and let her mind wander as she got her breath back. She started to draw up a list in her mind of the pros and cons of taking the new position. It didn't take long for her to realize that they were in equal measure. She would lose her new found friends here, but some would hopefully transfer too and Jeremy was already in LA. It had only been the last two months that she had seen her changes come to fruition and had stopped hearing George's name mentioned at all. However, by starting up a new office, Emersyn would not have to change anything. She could implement from the beginning how she wanted things run. She had finally found her feet in the role in Austin, but she did love a challenge and transferring would certainly be that.

For each con, there was a pro, but she was no closer to feeling like either choice was the right one. Emersyn turned off the treadmill and grabbed a towel to wipe her face as she made her way back to the house. She knew she was avoiding one main factor. Arlo. Was he a pro or a con?

The water felt great as she stood in the shower, washing her hair and just letting her mind think of Arlo without fighting it. Typically, she would push those thoughts away, but today was different. Today she had to be honest with herself. No more hiding from the pull the man had on her; no more pretending she didn't find him desirable. It was time to confront it and figure out what she wanted to do about it... if anything.

Throwing on a pair of ripped jeans, tie-died, blue kerchief top, and woven platform sandals, she put on a hint of lip gloss and mascara and finished the look by running her fingers through her wet, burgundy hair to bring out the natural wave. As she sat and ate her omelet, she thought hard about what she wanted to do regarding Arlo. *Why don't you just sleep with him and get him out of your system?* Emersyn rinsed her plate and put it in the sink. *Where did that come from?* she thought. *It's not the worst idea you have ever had.* She hated to admit it, but the idea appealed to her on a base level. She wanted to sleep with him; she dreamt about it often enough that she couldn't deny it.

Before Emersyn could rethink the idea or talk herself out of it, she grabbed the keys to her car and yelled to Harvey, "I'm going out. No clue when I will be back."

The sound of the sports car coming to life always made her grin with pleasure. She let the engine idle for a moment longer while she searched her phone for the text from Jaya that gave her Arlo's address. Emersyn noted that it was just before 11:00 a.m. Surely, he would be awake and have gotten rid of the woman in the red dress by this time of day. *I guess I'll find out. No backing out now.*

It only took twenty minutes to reach Arlo's address and locate the right apartment. Emersyn knocked on the door and waited. Trying not to fidget as she did. After a few moments, she knocked a little louder. It hadn't dawned on her until now that he might not be home at all. Her stomach twisted as she thought of all the places he might be and with who.

—◆—

Arlo

Arlo groaned as he rolled over and opened one eye to look at what time it was. It was just after 9:00 a.m., and he had only gotten around five hours sleep. His teeth were fuzzy and his tongue felt gross, his headache from last night had returned with a vengeance, and he refused to acknowledge that he had a hangover. Arlo went to the bathroom, splashed water on his face, and brushed his teeth before heading to the kitchen to find something to help with the headache. He grabbed his phone on the way through to discover that while he had been in the bathroom a text had come through.

R: Just tell her!

A: I'll think about it.

R: Stop thinking and do. Make her listen.

Arlo looked at the message and groaned as last night's conversation came back to him. Arlo had explained his growing infatuation with Emersyn and that due to her pushing him had rediscovered a passion for his work. Ray had immediately told him to take a chance with the girl and asked why hadn't he already done something about it. Arlo had to then fess up about the mess he had created in LA and that Emersyn had not been willing to hear him out.

In true Ray fashion, he had bluntly asked Arlo if he was ready to make a fool of himself for a girl because that's the only way he was going to get her to see past the player he had become. Arlo had tried to deny that he was a player because he didn't like the connotations that came with that word, but maybe that is what the world, and especially Emersyn, saw him as.

The fridge beeped at him as he realized he had been standing in front of it with the door open for too long. Arlo couldn't be bothered cooking, so poured himself a bowl of muesli and made himself his morning coffee before heading to the couch to eat, watch TV, and wait for the painkillers to kick in. Without meaning to, he dozed on and off for an hour before finally shaking himself awake and remembering that he had to go get his car that he had left at the bar the night before.

It was almost 10:45 a.m. by the time the Uber turned up to take him to his car and Arlo was feeling like his normal self. As he reached his car and got in and turned it on, his phone notified him of a text. He didn't have to look to know who it would be. Not knowing why, but suddenly feeling like it was now or never, he muttered under his breath, "Fine, Ray. I will go and tell her how I feel."

Before he could chicken out, he pulled the car out into the Saturday shopping and sports traffic and headed towards Emersyn's mansion. It didn't take him long to reach the landscaped, curved driveway and he chose to park under a tree on the far side of the circular area, bypassing the garage area so no one could be blocked in.

As he got to the beautifully carved double front doors he paused. *You didn't think this through very well, did you?* he thought. *What happens if the guy she was with last night slept over? I guess you'll find out.* He raised his hand and knocked on the door. *No backing out now.*

It didn't take long for her butler to open the door. "Hello, sir?"

"Hi, I'm Arlo, I work with Emersyn. I'm hoping I can talk to her."

"I remember you from the party. I am sorry to inform you that Miss Emersyn isn't home at present."

Arlo felt gutted. He had thought of every scenario on the way over but this one.

Chapter 26

Emersyn

Emersyn warred between being embarrassed about turning up at Arlo's door on impulse, being grateful that he wasn't there, and somewhere deep down that she wasn't willing to acknowledge, a little disgruntled that he wasn't there. She pulled her car into the garage and closed the remote door, and headed into the house via a side entrance. "I'm back," she called out as she dropped her keys and bag on the foyer table.

"Miss Emersyn, you rushed out so quickly. Is everything alright?" Harvey walked into the foyer and looked at her, concern etched on his face.

"Yes, everything is fine. I gave in to my feelings and went to see Arlo, but he wasn't there. Probably for the best..." Her voice trailed off. She didn't confide that she had been planning on going to bed with him in the hope that that would get him out of her system and give her a clear mind to make her decision.

"Why for the best?" Harvey prompted. They had been together for so long that the normal employee, employer protocols didn't always apply, like the movie watching and the pointed questions on occasion.

"He has been avoiding me at work," she admitted. "Mmm... the more I think about it, the more the idea seems silly now."

"You went to my house?" a deep voice from behind her asked.

She would know that voice anywhere. Emersyn glared at Harvey for not warning her that Arlo was in her house and could hear their conversation. Harvey just grinned, winked, and left the room. "I'll be in the kitchen if anyone needs me."

"You went to my house?" Arlo moved closer.

Emersyn turned around and took in the beauty of the man she dreamt about. He wore tan pants, matching leather shoes, and a black polo shirt that showed off his biceps. "You weren't home." *Well, that may be the stupidest thing you have ever said,* she told herself.

Arlo didn't laugh. "No, I was here, looking for you."

Almost involuntarily, Emersyn took a step toward him just as he took a step to her. This brought them close enough that she could smell his divine aftershave and see the flecks of gold in his brown eyes. She noted a small scar above his eyebrow and briefly wondered how he had got it. He slowly moved his hand up to take hers and she impulsively moved backward toward the staircase.

"Not this time," he muttered and followed her.

"What are you doing?" she asked as she slowly took two steps back, up the stairs. It was the first time she didn't need to look up into his face, as they were now on the same level.

His handsome Spanish face looked serious as he took the first step on the curved staircase. "I am hoping to get some answers." Emersyn took another step upwards and Arlo followed. "Why did you go to my house?"

Two more steps each.

"I don't know," Emersyn lied.

Another step.

"I don't believe you. You don't do anything without calculating the risks."

"You make me sound cold."

Three more steps and she was at the center section of the staircase. She quickly moved to the other side and continued backwards up the next step.

He followed.

"Not cold. Just cautious."

Emersyn couldn't argue with that. "I decided to give you what you want," she blurted.

They both took two more steps.

Arlo raised his eyebrows. "And what exactly do you think I want?"

Instead of answering, she took another step and changed tactic. "Why are you here, Arlo?"

That made him pause and gave her the chance to move up several more steps. She knew she was nearing the top and wasn't sure what she would do when they both reached it.

"I came to tell you that you need to hear me. You need to understand how sorry I am." His voice was sincere and his eyes begged her to listen.

"What are you sorry for?"

"I am sorry for putting you in the position I put you in in LA. I should never have slept with Pascal, even if she was single. It was completely wrong and I have no excuse."

Emersyn smiled despite herself. He had finally understood that she was upset because his choices had affected others and he was no longer making excuses for it. She took two more steps and realized that she had come to the top of the stairs. It was time to make a decision. Emersyn looked at his serious face, his strong nose, heavy eyebrows, and perfect cupid lips and her core responded. Her heart pounded and her breath became shallow as he took the final steps and closed the gap between them. She didn't step back.

For the first time since she had learned of Nicolai's betrayal, she put her fears aside and allowed her vulnerability to be seen. "Why have you been avoiding me?" she asked.

He lifted his hand and slowly pushed back a few strands of her hair, tucking them behind her ear. "Because you told me to," he whispered.

"I did?" Emersyn was confused. "I don't remember that."

His hand slid from her hair, down her shoulder, then arm, and finally, he took her hand. She didn't pull away. "You told me that you didn't need anything from me." He sounded sad.

Emersyn reached up with her free hand and cupped his neck, running her thumb along his cleanly shaven jaw. "I lied. I was drunk and wanted you, and then Eva was there doing up her dress and I lashed out."

Arlo's eyes widened as he finally heard the truth. "Eva and I..." he began, but Emersyn cut him off.

"I don't want to talk about Eva."

"Why did you go to my house, Emersyn?"

The conversation had come full circle. "To do this." She moved her hand from his neck and up into his hair, just like in her dream, and pulled his lips down to hers. The kiss was soft and sweet but turned to heated passion in an instant. She wouldn't deny her need for him any longer and she tugged on his hand and pulled him toward her bedroom.

Arlo followed her along the corridor and whistled softly as he entered her room. She didn't let go of his hand as she guided him toward the over-sized bed, her intentions clear. Emersyn sat on the side of the bed and took her shoes off, Arlo followed suit. She smiled at him and pulled her kerchief top over her head; he returned the smile and pulled his black polo off too. Emersyn grinned and stood and undid her button and zip, while he again copied her, but this time he stopped her from going any further. "Here, let me do that." His voice was husky.

"Be my guest." She held her hands up as if to surrender, which in a way she was.

As they both stood facing each other, Arlo reached out and put his hands on her hips, drawing her to him, and he lowered his head to kiss her. Their lips joined and sensations she had long held in burst like a dam. Emersyn opened her lips and flicked her tongue softly across his lower lip before sliding it along his tongue and twirling it around his mouth. He groaned, in turn making her open her mouth further to consume him. She felt him tug her pants over her hips, taking her panties with them.

Arlo kissed and nipped at her neck and down along her collarbone as he bent to pull her jeans further down. Soon she stood there in only her white laced bra, slightly quivering as he continued to kiss and bite a trail down her torso. Arlo knelt and as he peppered her pelvic bone in soft kisses, he lifted her leg and moved it over his shoulder. Emersyn held onto his shoulder with one hand while the other hand plunged into his short, curly hair to steady herself.

Her emerald eyes grew wide with pleasure as he licked her, his tongue running over her clit before taking her into his mouth and sucking. Emersyn bit her lip and dropped her head back as she became lost in the pleasure of the moment. All thought gone; replaced with nothing but the soft alternating sucking and licking of Arlo's rough tongue against her sensitive spot. Heat rushed to her core as her pleasure built and she could no longer hold back the soft sounds she always made when she was going to climax. The tightening grew, until without warning she exploded and dug her nails into Arlo's shoulder to keep herself upright as her legs shook and threatened to crumble. She was breathing heavily as Arlo unhooked her leg from his shoulder and slowly made his way back up her body, kissing her flat stomach and heaving chest as she fought to stop her legs from giving it out.

Arlo reached around her and undid the clasp of her bra, freeing her breasts before he claimed them with his hands, cupping each one and slowly rubbing his thumbs across the nipples. His mouth finally made its way back to her and they shared a passionate kiss before he took her by surprise and pushed her backward onto the bed. Emersyn laughed as she landed on the soft surface, but her thoughts turned lustful as she watched the handsome man peel his tan pants off, exposing his hard cock. He expertly removed a condom from his wallet and rolled it on as Emersyn wiggled further up the bed. He smiled in a predatory fashion as he crawled onto the bed and took hold of her legs, pulling them apart as he moved up.

Emersyn would have liked for him to stand still for a few moments longer so she could admire his hard abs and perfect V, but she happily settled for watching his upper body and bicep muscles ripple as he crawled towards her. He came to a stop when the head of his cock rested on her opening and he kissed her hard, demanding that her tongue join his. She moved her hips a fraction in the hope he would enter her, but he continued to just rest against her. He lowered his chest onto hers and the contact was beautiful—she had missed this. The intimacy of being naked and exposed, allowing your want to overwhelm all other thought.

A soft grunt escaped Arlo as Emersyn ran her fingernails along his spine and pushed a little harder with her hips. Inch by inch he entered her, filling her in every way, and the sensation was glorious. She rocked her hips upwards to meet him until they were joined with no space between them. Emersyn drew her knees up, allowing him deeper access and she felt her muscles tighten as her climax grew. Arlo withdrew as slowly as he had entered her and Emersyn spiraled into sensation as he slowly picked up the speed and intensity.

Emersyn pulled his head down toward her and kissed his neck and nibbled the lobe of his ear before sweeping her tongue along the outer ridge. She was rewarded with another low grunt from Arlo. As their orgasms mounted, Arlo broke their kiss and pulled his head far enough away that he could look into her eyes. Emersyn was mesmerized by the openness she saw, his longing exposed, and maybe something deeper. Neither blinked for those final moments as they rocked together before she and then he climaxed, bodies shuddering and backs arching, only breaking eye contact when he lowered his head to kiss the tip of her nose.

⸻◦◦◦⸻

Arlo

"Why now?" asked Emersyn as she pulled on an old t-shirt and settled back on the bed and snuggled up beside Arlo.

Arlo wound her hair around his hand. He loved the silkiness and smell of it as it slid through his fingers. "I don't understand the question." He was having trouble focusing on their conversation when she kept gently playing with the hair on his chest.

"Why did you decide today was the day you would turn up and insist I listen to you?" She bent down and kissed his nipple.

The conversation was not going to go far if she kept doing things like that. "It's silly. It doesn't matter anyway." He kissed the top of her head.

Emersyn sat up and stared at him. "It matters to me."

He looked into the green eyes, that from the first time he had met her, had mesmerized him. "I was jealous."

Arlo watched her frown, her usually smooth forehead creased with cute lines. "What would you have to be jealous about?" She genuinely sounded confused.

He pulled himself up a little higher on the bed and pulled her back down to cuddle against him. "I saw you on your date last night and wanted to know why, after all this time of rejecting me and Jaya always assuring me that you haven't dated at all since you arrived here, that you finally go on a date with him?" He said it in one long breath.

"Hang on, what?" She sat back up and turned to look at him. "I wasn't on a date last night. That was Arthur Chalmers you saw me with. If you hadn't have rushed out with your date you would have seen Henry Tran return to the table. It was a work meeting."

"My date? What are *you* talking about?"

"The woman is the tight red dress," she said, and it sounded almost like an accusation.

It took him a minute to understand who she was referring to. He started to laugh at the whole situation. "I was there picking up dessert alone. I saw you and panicked and knocked over the tray, the lady in the red dress was also waiting for food and just nice enough to help clean up the mess I made."

"So, your date was waiting in the car or at home?"

He sat up and caressed her face, tracing down her straight nose to her thinly set lips. "Emersyn, I haven't been on a date in months." He leaned in and kissed her. "You were right to avoid me, I just saw you as a challenge at first." He smiled sadly at her. "I was toxic to the women I was sleeping with, but mostly to myself." Arlo settled back against the luxuriously padded headboard once more and brought her with him.

"When did it change? Why was I no longer a challenge?"

"I think when you told me on the balcony that you wouldn't survive me. You looked so scared and vulnerable." He kissed her head. "I realized that even though I never meant to play with anyone's emotions, I could always justify it because I claimed to everyone that I was being honest, but I still was just being selfish."

"Why do it, though?" Her voice was almost timid. There was pain he didn't understand behind that question.

"It started at first as an ego thing. I realized that by listening to women they would give me what I wanted. It turns out that I didn't know what I wanted. I thought I wanted a different relationship than my parents; they are never affectionate toward each other and I was not mature enough to see depth in their love." He took a breath and exhaled it, astounded that he was willing to expose himself in a way to a woman that he never had before. "I wanted more than my friends in high school, I didn't want to settle as I perceived that they were willing to do. I wanted to stand out from the crowd and be the best at everything. The best at my job, the best at getting beautiful women to say yes, the best in my year at school. It turns out being the best doesn't make you the best." Arlo closed his eyes and waited for the recriminations to begin. He had told her all the bad things about himself and now he would pay the price.

He felt her move and couldn't bring himself to open his eyes, to see the disgust that would be on her face. Arlo's eyes flew open as he felt her lips on his. He saw the lust in her eyes and was bewildered by the response, though he instantly hardened in reply.

"It turns out that I find a man who can own his faults an incredible turn on." Emersyn pulled her t-shirt off and straddled him, her hands lay flat on his pecs. She kissed him more urgently and his tongue sought hers. "You got another condom?" she asked as they broke apart.

He didn't want to sound his usual self so answered without the practiced charm. "Yes."

"Good. I need a shower," she answered as she moved off him, exposing his erection. "Grab that condom and follow me."

Arlo scrambled off the bed, watching the naked Emersyn open a set of double doors and her perfect ass disappear through them. Without further thought, other than that he would follow that gorgeous rear end anywhere, he got the condom and walked into the most expensive bathroom he had ever encountered. For a minute, he worried that Emersyn Cole was out of his league in every way before he shook the self-doubt and moved to the walk-in shower to discover that Emersyn looked just as hot with her beautiful burgundy hair wet and slicked back. She held in her hand a large soaped up sponge and crooked her index finger at him. Arlo didn't need to be asked twice.

The water was wonderful as it poured over his shoulders. The double shower head allowed both of them to remain in the stream of the water while they kissed. Emersyn ran the soapy sponge over his back and down over his ass before breaking the kiss and washing his chest and abs. She abandoned the sponge, making sure there was still plenty of soap on her hands before she took hold of his cock and slid her hand up and down his length. Arlo groaned with pleasure as she increased the tightness of her grip and rubbed the head with her thumb. He began to feel his muscles tighten and knew she needed to stop soon or he would pump his seed into her hand. Taking control, he took a step back and out of the water, drying his hands on the towel nearby so he could rip the condom packet open.

Emersyn's hands were slowly moving along his shoulders and down his back, he shivered as her nails dug into his skin. Arlo was finding it hard to focus as she followed the trail of nails with tiny bites and licks. He turned and pulled her to him, kissing her full lips while his hands did their own exploring. He couldn't wait any longer, his erection demanded him to stop playing and enter her.

Arlo turned Emersyn around and moved her closer to the shower wall, he stood behind her and took her hands, placing them on the wall. As he moved his hands back over her arms, he put one leg between hers and gently moved them apart, being careful she didn't slip. The sight of her spread-eagle, waiting for him was hot. Emersyn moaned as his hands cupped her breasts and he played with her nipples. The sound was delicious. He kissed the nape of her neck as he bent his knees for a better angle and entered her. The feeling of her warmth enveloping him was incredible and he fought for control as his body craved to pound into her while his heart told him to make sure she was ready for that.

His large hands covered hers, keeping her in place as he increased the speed. Emersyn responded by standing on her tippy toes and pushing her hips back and up against him. Arlo grunted with rising pleasure as he slid in and out. He kept one hand over hers against the wall as he let go of her other hand and brought his hand down to her stomach before crawling it over her groomed pubic hair and finding her clit within her perfect folds. Emersyn let out the softest groan and dropped her head as his fingers started to apply pressure and move in a circular motion. He slowed his thrusts as he concentrated on giving her pleasure while maintaining his knife-edge balancing act of not ramping up his speed and spilling his seed before she was complete.

Arlo felt her body tighten in anticipation and began to thrust harder, his own core demanding to be satisfied. Her panting increased, matching his ragged breaths, and as she shuddered against his hand his body surged and his orgasm exploded from him. He moved his hand up to her stomach and held her against him as he slowly moved in and out, his legs shaking in the aftermath of their passion.

As Arlo kissed the back of her neck and settled his body against hers, his mind began to mutter at him that she was the one. That if he weren't such an idiot, they could have been doing this for months. *Yes, but back then you would have bedded her and moved on. Now you know how special she is and that you want more. So, don't wreck it.*

"Arlo." Emersyn speaking his name stopped all thought.

"Mmmm." He nibbled her earlobe.

"Let me go so I can turn and kiss you." Her voice was strained.

Alarm bells went off as he pulled out with reluctance and let go of the hand that had her pinned to the wall. The arm that held her around the waist continued to hold her as she turned to face him. Her beautiful eyes searched his, they were looking for something. He bent his head and kissed her as he gathered her tightly against him.

Chapter 27

Emersyn

Sunday, the day of rest, the day to enjoy the simple pleasures of life. *If only that were the case today,* thought Emersyn. She sat in the breakfast nook of her kitchen, opposite Arlo, and ate scrambled eggs on toast that he had just cooked for the both of them. She smiled warmly and fought the urge to lure him back to her bedroom while her inner thoughts avoided the turmoil she had created. *Sleeping with him was supposed to get him out of your system, you stupid girl, not settle him under your skin.*

Arlo looked up from his eggs and winked at her. "Do you have a nickname?"

"My mother and a few close friends call me Emmy."

"Emmy," he spoke it aloud. "Emmy, I've been wondering about something."

Emersyn was on guard immediately. Would he ask her questions that she wasn't prepared to answer about Nicolai? She didn't want to ruin their weekend with thoughts of him. "What?"

"Why were you out with Arthur Chalmers on Friday night when no one even knows he is in town? I've met the man briefly once when I first began, which is why I didn't recognize him, and here you are having dinner with him."

"They offered me a new position," she said.

"That's great. You deserve it, you work so hard." Arlo appeared truly happy for her.

"In LA," Emersyn added.

"Oh."

Silence grew between them as they finished their breakfast. "I wasn't expecting for you to say that," he admitted.

"I wasn't expecting the offer. They are opening an office in LA and want me to head the accounting team," she explained.

"That's wonderful." His enthusiasm didn't ring true this time. "I will miss you."

She didn't know what made her say it and the moment it was out she wished she could retract it. "I'm sure Eva will help you miss me a little less."

"Eva?" He looked confused.

"Yes, you know. The one you went swimming with in my pool at my party," Emersyn reminded him.

"Emmy, I didn't go swimming with her. I've done nothing with her but give her a lift home, which turned into a pain because when we got to her place, she discovered that she couldn't find her keys. I let her sleep at my place, in the spare room, and then, well... you know the rest. The keys were found by the pool."

"You had no shoes on and she was zipping up her dress when she walked in. I was drunk, but I know what I saw," insisted Emersyn.

"After your rebuke on the balcony and watching you dance without a care that night, I went to find somewhere quiet to get away from everyone. I was just dangling my feet in the pool when she arrived sans dress and took a swim." He looked at her as if willing her to believe him. "Nothing happened. She gave it her best shot, but nothing happened." He reached across and took her hand. "Are you going to take the job?"

"I don't know. It was less complicated on Friday night."

"Don't take me into account. You do what's right for you." He squeezed her hand and then let go.

What did he mean by that? She didn't get a chance to ask as he stood up, grabbed the empty plates, and took them to the sink.

"I've got to go. I have this tyrannical person in accounting that makes sure I am always showing up with my best ideas on a Monday morning," he said lightly.

Emersyn came around the kitchen bench, she had other ideas of how she would prefer to get ready for work. "I'm sure this demanding person can be persuaded to cut you a bit of slack." Untying her wrap dress, she pushed him up against the bench and kissed him.

Arlo disentangled her arms from around his neck and gently pushed her away. "Sorry, Emmy, but I really have to go." He kissed the top of her head and turned away.

Her face blushed as she tied her dress and took a step back. "No problem. I'll see you out."

Things had grown rapidly awkward between them and Emersyn was at a loss as to why. She walked him through her house and to the foyer when she opened one of the doors for him. "I had a great time, thanks for stopping by." She tried to make light of the situation with the throwaway line.

"Emmy, congrats again on the job offer." Arlo smiled down at her, reached out and touched her cheek, and walked away.

Emersyn closed the door before he could see the hurt she felt and swore loudly. "What the hell?"

Her head spun with a myriad of emotions that now played through her mind. She felt stunned by the way the conversation had turned. He had gone from caring and sincere, to finding out about the job offer and almost running out of there. It hurt. Emersyn had finally opened up to a man again and shown her true self and he had repaid that trust by disappearing. A horrid thought rose to the surface and though she tried to avoid it, it would not leave her alone. A little voice whispered in her head, *maybe he played you all along, he got what he wanted and when things got real, he ran. Admit that he had to work harder for you, but you caved in the end, just like all the rest of them.* Was that it or was she just overreacting and he had told the truth and he just needed to go? *What did it matter? You only slept with him to get him out of your system...right?* Emersyn didn't want to admit how much she had been kidding herself.

Chapter 28

Emersyn

Monday morning had dawned dreary and wet and with no decision made for Emersyn and the job offer. She had spent the remainder of Sunday with her pros and cons list and still wasn't certain on which side Arlo fell. Emersyn needed to talk to him, to find out where she stood. If she did turn out to be a conquest and nothing more, then she would be bitterly disappointed in herself for falling for another liar, but if he was being honest with her about not having dated for months and that it was only her he was interested in then she would consider all options. Her career was important to her, but after you watch someone die at an early age, you tend to understand that many things are just as important. Her mother had shown her to enjoy the moments in between the big achievements because, in the end, the moments are what make you laugh and keep you going when things get hard. She had almost forgotten that.

Emersyn was surprised to see so many people in the lobby as she came through the revolving glass doors. She was relieved to discover Arlo standing near the lift as if he were waiting for her. He gave a hesitant wave and half smile. She made her way over to him, only for him to be intercepted by Eva. Normally Emersyn would have been put off by this and gone straight to the elevator, today she straightened her shoulders, told herself to trust him when he said nothing had happened between them, and ketp walking toward him.

Emersyn overheard him asking Eva as she approached, "How was your weekend?"

"It was great. My friends and I went to a new club that opened and I met a great guy. I'm hoping he rings and asks me out," she gushed.

"Sounds like fun." He turned and looked at Emersyn. "Good morning, Emersyn. Did you have a good weekend?" His face was serious.

"Wonderful. I managed to tick a few things off my list I'd been meaning to get to, though it ended too quickly." She smiled at the both of them. "I heard what Eva said about hers. So what about you, Arlo, how was your weekend?"

"It was surprising and I managed to get a few workouts in," he answered with a straight face.

Emersyn was amused by his answer and felt a little more on sure footing that his run out may have been in her head. As more of the crowd cleared, Emersyn was shocked to see Samantha with Sahara being pulled behind her, stalking her way towards her. Fear gripped her and she looked around for somewhere to go so that Samantha wouldn't create a scene and embarrass Emersyn in front of her colleagues. Which she assumed would be the whole point of turning up to her work with her child in tow.

The elevator doors opened and Emersyn all but pushed Eva and Arlo toward the lift. "You go up, I just remembered that I left something in my car. I'll have to get it. I'll catch you both later."

"I need to talk to you about the new proposal so I'll just walk with you if you don't mind?" Arlo said.

Eva shrugged and stepped into the lift. "Cool, I'll see you later."

This time Emersyn forcibly pushed Arlo toward the doors. "I don't have time to talk. I'll catch you later." She looked over her shoulder to find Samantha had almost reached her.

"But—"

"Arlo, just go." Emersyn didn't give him the chance to say more, she spun on her heel and walked rapidly away from the elevator.

She thought she heard the words, "too much" and "hot and cold" hover in the air before the lift doors closed on Eva and Arlo.

"Where do you think you're going?" Samantha asked in a cool, loud voice.

Emersyn closed her eyes briefly and once again cursed Nicolai for his affair with the entitled socialite. Emersyn moved to where they wouldn't be standing in the center of the flow of foot traffic that was coming in to start their day. *Please don't let Arthur or Henry come in now*, she prayed to whatever god would listen. Resigned to the confrontation that was about to occur, Emersyn turned to face Samantha. "What do you want?" she asked in a quiet, even tone.

"I want what's owed to me," Samantha said loudly, making several people turn around.

"I don't owe you anything, Samantha." Emersyn refused to be dragged into the drama.

"Oh, you do and you will pay," she warned aggressively.

"Did you just threaten me?"

Samantha pulled Sahara in front of her. "Look at my baby." She picked up Sahara and turned her to face Emersyn. "She is going hungry and wearing old clothes, while you sit in your mansion you bought with the money you stole."

Emersyn looked at Sahara, who looked scared of her mother yelling, but otherwise her clothes were clean, designer labelled, and her adorable cheeks were chubby and well fed. "I told you before, I took no money from Nicolai. I don't care what he is telling you."

Samantha's face reddened with rage as she was being denied what she believed to be hers. "Give me a hundred thousand and I will go away. Otherwise, I will turn up here every day and tell everybody what type of person you are, denying a child their rightful money from their father." She was yelling now.

People had stopped to watch the commotion and Emersyn knew that at any minute someone would start recording it on their phone. "Excuse me, Miss Cole, would you and your friend like to take this into the privacy of the security office over here?" One of the security guards interrupted the yelling. Emersyn watched as he efficiently took hold of Samantha's elbow and propelled her to the door, as if he was just escorting her. "This way, Ma'am."

Emersyn was about to follow when she was intercepted by the other security guard. "I have called the police. They won't be long," he told her. "Stay with Russell, he'll make sure you are safe."

"Thank you," she said softly before she moved to catch up with the fuming Samantha.

Russell was calm as he showed them into a room and followed them in. "It might be best if you sat on either side of the table." They were in a room that reminded Emersyn of the interrogation rooms that you saw on cop shows. It was bare, aside from a security camera up in a ceiling corner and a table with a few chairs. Russell indicated for Samantha and Sahara to take seats on the opposite side of the table to the door, which he locked and pulled a chair to sit in front of. Emersyn sat on the same side as him.

"Do you know what this bitch did?" Samantha yelled at Russell as soon as they were all seated.

"Ma'am, please don't speak about Miss Cole like that."

Samantha ignored him and continued to yell. "She took all of her husband's money when she left, just to make me pay for having an affair with him and getting pregnant." She sat back in her chair and glared at Emersyn and Russell. "Can you believe that?"

"No, Ma'am, that is difficult to believe."

Emersyn knew that he was telling her that he didn't believe it, but Samantha was on a roll and misconstrued the comment. "I know, right? Who would do that?" Sahara began to fuss and Samantha put a movie for her to watch on her phone. "I warn you, Emersyn, I will get what is mine."

"And I have told you before that if you want money from Nicolai then speak to Nicolai or your lawyer, I don't have his money to give you." Emersyn was exasperated with the conversation that kept going around in circles. "You need to stop threatening me."

There was a polite knock on the door and Russell stood to answer it. He stepped back and let the two police officers in. "What is going on here?" Samantha demanded.

"Ma'am, please calm down. There has been a complaint made that you were heard to make threats to someone and we have come to investigate."

Samantha picked up Sahara and put her on her lap like she was a shield. Emersyn was sickened with the gesture. "I have made no threats."

Russell coughed politely. "I have heard her demand money and make several threats."

"You can't do this to me," Samantha announced.

Everyone ignored her. One of the officers turned to Emersyn. "Would you be willing to make a statement and then we can take her down to the station and you can get back to work?"

Emersyn looked at Samantha and decided that she had been given enough chances to understand that Emersyn was not responsible for her financial troubles. It was time for her to grow up. "I just need to send a text to my people upstairs to let them know I'm running a bit late and then I will make a statement."

Arlo

As soon as Arlo had left Emersyn on Sunday, he had regretted it. He had called himself names all the way home and had spent the remainder of the afternoon wondering what had made him react so poorly. She had been offered a fantastic job opportunity and his response had been to run away because, if he was honest, his ego got hurt. Arlo had had to face that he would not be offered this chance because of his choices in LA and he would just have to deal with that, but why did Emersyn have to pay for his choices? He had had a wonderful twenty-four hours with her and he had ruined it. *All that talk of honesty to her and in the end, you ran rather than tell her how you were feeling.* It seemed he still had a lot to learn. He was just hoping that she would still be willing to give him a chance. He was trying not to think about what he would do if she had decided to take the job.

Monday morning found him standing in the busy lobby of their office building, pretending to check messages on his phone while he secretly waited for Emersyn. As people came into the foyer and greeted colleagues and friends while moving to the lifts, he noticed a beautiful young woman with a toddler standing to one side; she appeared to be waiting for someone too.

He spotted the unmissable color of Emersyn's burgundy hair, all neatly tucked up in its customary bun for work. He watched her come through the revolving doors and head toward the lift, so he half lifted his hand in a wave and gave her a hesitant smile. Emersyn returned the smile and his mood lightened as he thought that perhaps he hadn't blown the whole thing by running away. Arlo was caught off guard when Eva abruptly stood before him. "Hey, Arlo."

Not now, Eva, he thought as he watched, hoping that Emersyn wouldn't bypass him. She seemed determined to greet him. "Hey Eva, how was your weekend?" he asked, not listening to her answer.

Emersyn joined them and smiled warmly and his heart did a tiny somersault.

"Sounds like fun," he replied to Eva without having heard a word she said. He looked directly at Emersyn and asked her how her weekend was.

"Wonderful. I managed to tick a few things off my list I'd been meaning to get to, though it ended too quickly."

Arlo struggled to keep his eyebrows from lifting at the meaning behind her remarks and answered her question about his weekend, with what he hoped was a straight face. But instead of finding his remarks amusing, her face paled and she began to usher them toward the open lift door, telling them that she had forgotten something and needed to go back to her car. Arlo was completely confused and wanted to talk to her so suggested he walk her back to the car so they could discuss an upcoming proposal.

"I don't have time to talk. I'll catch you later," she insisted

Arlo was determined to figure out what he had said to create the rapid change in demeanor. "But—"

She didn't allow him to finish. "Arlo, just go." Her voice was cold and angry and she turned around and left him standing there.

"Come on, Arlo. People are waiting," Eva said.

"That was a bit too much. She runs way too hot and cold sometimes," he announced as the doors closed. Emersyn was frustrating, and behavior like that made him second guess his choice. *Are you already looking for excuses?* he asked himself.

"Don't worry about it, Arlo, women behave strangely all the time," counseled one of the men in the lift. This earned him several glares from the female occupants and everyone settled into an awkward silence.

Arlo's phone pinged just as he was entering his office. "Good morning, Mrs. Beaulieu, how are you?"

"Good morning, Mr. Medina. I am well. How are you today?" She was shuffling papers and didn't look up.

"I am mystified, Mrs. Beaulieu, completely mystified."

"Wonderful, Mr Medina. Here are your messages. Your mother has called to ask you to contact her."

"That's odd." He took the messages and went into his office, enjoying the warmth of the sunlight that streamed through the window as he looked at his phone messages. A text from his mother telling him that it would be great if he could call home. Two messages from his mother in the space of fifteen minutes was unusual. He pressed the call button.

Tracy picked up immediately. "Hi Arlo, thanks for getting back to me."

"Hey, Mom, what's going on?"

"Now, I don't want you to worry, but your father went and had tests done last week and the doctor has called him in to discuss the results."

For someone who doesn't want me to worry she sounds pretty worried herself, he thought. "What did he have tests for?"

"Oh, one of his customers came into the warehouse the other week and commented that she was a skin specialist and that she didn't like the look of the mark on your father's cheek. She advised getting it checked out." Tracy was being vague on the specifics.

"Mom, what were the tests for?"

"He went to a specialist who checked his whole body. They were concerned with the one on his face and one on his shoulder, so they took a small biopsy."

"Mom." Arlo was becoming frustrated with her but knew she was upset and didn't want to push her.

"Melanoma. They think he has skin cancer. We will get the results today." Tracy sounded worried, but like she was pretending it was fine because you never upset the children.

"Can I speak with Papa?" he asked.

"Arlo, we have to go. The doctor is calling us in. I'll let you know as soon as we get out."

"Okay, love you." He hung up the call.

Arlo stood in his office and took in big, steadying breaths as the word cancer echoed in his head. He tried to focus on going through the rest of his messages, but nothing was registering. In the end, he just sat on his lounge and looked out the window, willing his mother to call him to tell him it was a false alarm. *It'll be fine,* he repeated to himself while he waited.

Finally, his mother got back to him, but only via text.

T: Hi Arlo. Yes, Doc says it is Melanoma, but got it early. Papa goes into surgery on Wednesday. Lots to organize, will ring you later today when we know more. Xox

A: K. Give Papa a hug for me. Ring me as soon as you can.

Arlo sat there for several more minutes, his mind jumped from Emersyn's mercurial mood to the shocking news that his father had skin cancer. How did his life become so complicated so quickly? *I need to go home.*

"Mrs. Beaulieu," he called through the door as he got up and went to his desk. Arlo began to pack a few things into his briefcase, but he decided that he would leave most of the work to Jaya; she was capable, and it would do her good to run the office for a while.

"Yes, Mr. Medina?" The perfectly groomed Mrs. Beaulieu opened the door.

"I need to get home now and will be taking a week or two off. Can you please book me on the first flight home and let the powers that be know that I am taking leave effective immediately?"

"Is everything okay?"

"There is some family stuff I have to take care of."

Within five minutes, Arlo was heading back downstairs and home to pack—his flight was leaving in two hours. He thought about letting Emersyn know what was happening, but after hearing the coldness in her voice he wasn't sure he should bother. Maybe he would do it when he got home and knew more about his father's illness.

———◆———

Emersyn

Humiliated, but trying to look composed, Emersyn left the small security guard's office, where she had just spent twenty minutes making a statement to the police regarding Samantha and her demands and threats. Fortunately, the morning crowd had dispersed and the lobby was mostly empty, with only people coming in for appointments milling around. She made her way to the lift and pressed the up button. As the door opened and she got in, her finger hovered over her floor before Emersyn decided to see Arlo and pressed his floor instead. She needed to tell him what was going on and ask him to forgive her strange behavior. She was nervous about letting him see her so vulnerable, but it was better than him thinking she was running hot and cold or too much, as that is what she had overheard.

The elevator doors hissed opened and she exited to find a group of people gathered at the end of the corridor, near Arlo and Jaya's offices. As she moved down the hallway, people began to look up and upon seeing her, scurried back to the offices and desks. A sick feeling was beginning to grow in her stomach as only Jaya and Mitchell waited in the now deserted office area.

"I'm off to get coffee, do either of you two want anything?" Mitchell announced as he moved past Emersyn.

"I'm good, thanks," replied Jaya.

"Nothing for me, thank you," answered Emersyn.

"What happened?" Jaya asked quietly, confirming that the gossip of the confrontation in the lobby had started circulating.

"I'll explain later. I need to talk with Arlo." Emersyn went to walk past Jaya and she caught her arm.

"He's not here, he's gone on leave. No one is saying much."

"What? He's gone?" Emersyn couldn't understand what she was being told. He had just left without contacting her? *That's how little care he has for you*, she thought. *Well, it looks like you got your answer.*

Jaya stared at her for a few minutes. "You didn't?" she groaned.

Emersyn didn't know what to say so she nodded.

Jaya gave her a quick hug, aware that people were probably watching, and then smiled sadly at her as she stepped back. "Want to tell me who the crazy lady in the lobby was?"

"My ex-husband had an affair with her and she became pregnant. He broke up with her when she told me what was going on. The asshole has told her that I took all his money when I divorced him so she keeps making a nuisance of herself and demanding I give her what she believes is hers." Emersyn's voice was hard as she explained.

"Was everything taken care of this morning?"

"Russell and the other security guard were amazing. They intervened and removed her from the lobby and called the police. I have made a statement and hopefully it will be enough for her to understand that she can't turn up and harass people."

"That must have been awful for you." Jaya gave her friend another hug.

"Is everyone talking about it?" Emersyn didn't like her private life being talked about, that's one of the reasons this job had been so appealing.

"Half are talking about you and half about Arlo and his sudden disappearance. Mrs. Beaulieu is very good at keeping his secrets and has only managed to tell me that I am in charge for at least a week." Jaya pouted.

"I have to go, but we need to have lunch. There is more I need to tell you." Emersyn wanted to talk to Jaya about the job offer and what had happened on the weekend.

"I don't know if I can make lunch, I have a meeting with Henry Tran this morning."

Emersyn smiled. That could mean that they were going to offer Jaya a new job too. Her name hadn't been brought up when they discussed her thoughts on people on Friday night, but maybe they had changed their minds? It would be great if Jaya was offered a position in the LA office too. "Okay, that's cool. Maybe dinner instead?"

"Dinner works," said Jaya. "I'll text you."

"Good luck in your meeting." Emersyn waved as she walked away.

It didn't take long for Emersyn to reach her floor, and by the time she got to her office she was angry. All the calm she had displayed as she walked through the office had dissipated and her hurt, fear, and frustration had grown. Emersyn felt humiliated. She had allowed Arlo in and he had repaid her trust by taking off without any word, for what she finds out could be more than a week. It was now obvious that he didn't care if she took the job or not. And now she was again the center of office gossip because of Samantha's hysterics and demands in the busy lobby this morning. Tears burned the back of her throat as she settled into her desk chair and turned on her computer.

There was a polite tap on her door.

"Yes?" answered Emersyn.

Penny, the accounting department's general secretary, opened the door. "Mr. Tran would like to know if you are available now for a quick meeting."

"Sure, tell him I'll be right in," Emersyn said.

Penny closed the door and Emersyn got up and checked her reflection to make sure she looked confident and in control. Happy that the stress of the morning didn't show in the mirror, Emersyn grabbed a notebook and paper, just in case she needed to make notes, and headed to Henry's office on the other side of the same floor.

As Emersyn arrived, Henry's PA was coming out of his office. She held the door open for her.

Henry was sitting on a black leather couch holding a teacup, while Arthur Chalmers sat in a matching black leather armchair sipping from a mug of coffee. The office was twice as big as Arlo's with a brilliant view. They both shook her hand before Henry offered her a seat and hot beverage.

Arthur got straight to the point. "Before we can start our recruitment of anyone else, we need to know your answer. Have you decided yet on the job offer?"

Emersyn hadn't decided until she had reached her office five minutes before and realized that there was no life for her here. Sleeping with Arlo had been a costly mistake to her heart and career and Samantha had added to the want to start fresh. "I have decided. I would love to take the job, but I have a proviso that I can leave by the end of this week." This way she would be gone before Arlo returned.

"That can be arranged, I'm sure. There is much to be done and I'll be happy for you to get out there ASAP and do some supervising," Henry said.

Chapter 29

Arlo

"The doctor says I'm going to be fine," Luis assured Arlo. "I just need to take the week off work, and I won't be able to lift anything at the warehouse for a few weeks, and I have to wear a hat when I go outside."

Tracy gave her husband a smug look before squeezing his arm. Arlo knew that she had been telling him for years to wear sunscreen, that it didn't matter that his skin was more tanned than hers. Luis gave a surrendering smile back. Arlo was again struck by how different his parents' relationship was to what he had assumed it to be.

"But you have cancer," countered Arlo.

"Yes, but they caught it really early, thanks to the customer who told me to check it out," his father patiently explained for the third time.

Tracy looked seriously at her son. "Arlo, why did you come home so suddenly? I told you I would let you know later today once everything was arranged and clarified."

"Do I need an excuse to visit you guys?" He tried a different tactic. It didn't work.

"Arlo, has something happened at work?" his mother tried to guess.

"Ugghhh." Arlo stood and walked around the living room. "I don't know what's wrong with me. I panicked. You said cancer and I just got on a plane."

Both of his parents stood and came to him, they embraced him in a three-way hug and Arlo felt accepted in a way that had eluded him for so long. It was good to be home.

"I'm going into the warehouse today to get a few things organized before I have to take time off. Would you like to come with me?" Luis asked Arlo as they broke apart.

"That would be great, Dad. I haven't been to the place in years and I'd be happy to help out over the next week if I'm needed."

⸻◆⸻

Emersyn

Clothes were strewn all over the huge walk-in wardrobe as Emersyn attempted to decide what she was taking with her to LA immediately and what would be shipped later. *I'll probably need two to three weeks worth of clothes,* she mused as she put a silver trimmed, black blazer on the maybe pile. *I need to make a list.* Typically Emersyn had no trouble organizing her packing for trips. She always found it exciting to decide what to take as it always meant she was going somewhere new or special. This time just seemed overwhelming, and not for the first time since Emersyn had agreed to move yesterday morning did she wonder whether she had made the right decision.

Her phone rang. "Oh, thank goodness," she muttered. "Saved from myself." Emersyn looked at the caller. It was Jaya. "Hello."

"Hey, you busy Friday night?" Jaya didn't bother with any preamble.

"I was going to ask you the same thing?" replied Emersyn.

"Oh good, because we need to celebrate."

Emersyn was surprised by that, she assumed Jaya would be upset with her leaving. *I wonder who told her? Damn, I wanted to be the one to let her know that I'm going.* Emersyn was annoyed with herself for putting off telling Jaya now. "I thought you would be a little upset."

"Why would I be upset? I thought you might be upset?" countered Jaya.

"I think we are talking about two different things. Jaya, what do you want to celebrate, but you think I might be sad about?" asked Emersyn.

"I've been offered a job at the New York office," whooped Jaya.

"That is fantastic. Congratulations, no wonder you want to celebrate."

"So, what is your news? Hang on, I've just put it all together. I've been offered the same position I'm doing, but under a new guy because the Arlo equivalent in New York is heading to LA to start up the new office there." Jaya paused and then gasped. "You are going to LA too."

"Yes, but I leave Saturday and was hoping you could take me to the airport?"

"Saturday? Why so soon? I'm not leaving for a few more weeks," asked Jaya.

"I agreed to help interview the staff we are hiring out there and aiding Ruby in setting everything up. It's going to be a great challenge."

"I am thrilled for you. Double celebrations Friday night. What time do I have to get you to the airport?"

"I need to be there by 1:30 p.m.," Emersyn answered.

"Cool, I can do that. So, more importantly, where do you feel like going for your last night in Austin? Should we try somewhere new or go back to an old favourite?"

They reminisced about the last five months and all the great places they had tried. They decided to start the night somewhere they had always hoped to get to, but end it at one of their favourite places. After

Emersyn had hung up the phone she had realized that they had not discussed where Jaya would live in New York.

Emersyn had an idea. She was due to call her father and check in anyway. Emersyn rapidly scrolled through her phone until her father's number came up. She had no idea where he was in the world so trying to figure out if she was interrupting his sleep was pointless, he would always answer if he saw her ringing. The last time Emersyn had spoken to him he had been in Fiji, on some stunning tropical island.

After the fourth ring her father, Thomas, picked up the phone. "Hi, Emmy." His speech was slightly slurred, but Emersyn was used to it and ignored it. Her father would drink himself to death and it was something she had had to learn to cope with knowing.

"Hey, Dad, how are you?"

"I am getting by," was his standard answer. "How are you, Emmy?"

"I am great. I have some wonderful news for you." Emersyn tried to fill her voice with the excitement she should feel at the opportunity she was being given. "I am heading to LA to live and work. Chalmers and Tran were so impressed with what I have done in Austin that they want me to head the accounting department in the new office they are opening in LA."

"Emmy, that is amazing. I am so proud of you. Well done." Thomas stopped talking to have a drink.

Emersyn waited, pretending that she wasn't upset by it and that this was a normal, healthy relationship, where your father didn't ignore you for most of your life and you overlook his deadly drinking habits.

"Where will you live? I had Jeremy lease the LA property only a few months ago."

"Don't worry about it; I earn good money. I can find a really great house for Harvey and myself." Emersyn never asked her father for favors, so it was difficult to find the words. "Dad, I need something."

"Name it, Emmy."

"I have a dear friend who is moving to New York and I was wondering if the apartment is free? She can't pay the usual rates you would get, but I would like to help her for six months until she finds her feet," Emersyn explained.

"It is standing empty at the moment. The last lot moved out about two weeks ago. I'll let the studio know that it will be unavailable to hire for the next seven months. Does that suit you?"

"That is very considerate of you, Dad, thank you. Jaya has been a great friend to me and I would like to repay the favor." She waited for him to finish another long swig.

"It is my pleasure. It is only uppity actors and studio heads that use the place, it would be nice to know someone that will appreciate those park views."

Emersyn heard a female voice murmuring in the background and tried to ignore it.

"Emmy, I got to go. It was great to talk to you. I'll get the people that handle the New York apartment to email you everything tomorrow. Congrats on the job."

Before she had a chance to say good bye, the line disconnected. "Love you," she whispered into the phone.

Chapter 30

Arlo

The week had passed quickly, the operation had been a success, and the doctors were confident that they had got both Melanomas. Luis had recovered well, and had only stayed in the hospital overnight. It was now Saturday afternoon and Arlo could hear his parents laughing as they prepared a family feast because his sister, Santana, and her family would be joining them for dinner. It was rare that Arlo was home, so they were taking as many opportunities as they could to be all together.

Arlo had come to the uncomfortable conclusion that he had been running from something that didn't exist for the last ten years. What he had always understood his parents' relationship to be was only the surface because he had assumed that you had to show affection constantly to be, what he thought was, in true love. He had only now come to truly understand the depth of their affection and unconditional love. It would be an incredible feeling to just be who you were and still know that you would always be loved.

But I don't want to be tied down, he thought as he closed his laptop and grabbed his phone. *Tied down to boring and being tied to the person that accepts and loves you and you accept and love them are two very different things,* the wiser part of his brain reasoned. "I want adventure and fun and to experience living in different places," he muttered to himself as he tapped his phone and found Jaya's number. "What makes you think Emersyn wouldn't want those things? You might just need to talk to her about your wants and listen to her," he answered himself. A deeper part noted that he seemed to always be coming up with another reason for his choices.

Jaya picked up the call on the third ring. "Hello, Arlo." Her voice was cool.

"Hi, Jaya. How has your week been? I'm hearing great things when I check in with the team."

"What has been going on? Arlo, people have been interviewing for jobs at the new LA office and you haven't been here." Her voice hadn't softened.

"I knew about the job offers. I'm not being offered anything because of the Happy Girl situation—can't say I blame them." He pretended that it didn't sting to know he would probably have been offered the job if he hadn't have screwed that up. "You been offered something?" he asked, expecting her to say no. They made a great team and he doubted that the bosses would want to mess with that.

There was a pause. Shit, she *had* been offered something.

"They are doing a straight swap. You get the guy from New York who does my job and I get to try my talents out with the new person coming into the New York office."

"Where's Natalia going?" he asked, even though he knew the answer as soon as he asked the question.

"Natalia will launch the LA office in a month's time." Jaya's voice had warmed slightly.

"You deserve the chance to go to New York. You are going to learn so much there. It's a different type of environment I'm told." Arlo really was happy for Jaya. "When do I lose you?"

"Two weeks things will start to change. It gives everyone a chance to straighten their own affairs and find places to live as well as get any of the jobs they need to complete done." Jaya paused and Arlo could almost hear her decide if she wanted to ask the next question. "Are you okay? You left so quickly."

"Yes, I am sorry about that. Dad got diagnosed with skin cancer and I panicked. He's had surgery and he's healing as expected. He will make a full recovery," explained Arlo.

"Oh my goodness, I am so sorry to hear that. Arlo why didn't you tell someone? Why didn't you tell Emersyn?" asked Jaya.

By that last question Arlo knew that Emersyn had confided in Jaya about their weekend together. "All the reasons I had don't seem to matter anymore. And then it was like I waited too long and now I figure it's probably best to do it face to face when I get home tomorrow night."

"Oh, Arlo. It's too late."

"What do you mean?" Fear gripped him.

"She's gone. I dropped her at the airport an hour ago." Jaya sounded upset.

"Gone?" He was confused.

"Yes, gone. Between you running off without a word after she finally let you in and then the scene in the lobby that had everyone talking about her, she took the job on the condition she could finish up this week... before you got back, would be my guess."

Arlo felt like he was only understanding half the conversation. "There was a scene in the lobby? What are you talking about?"

"Yes, I am surprised no one has blabbed to you about it. A woman with a child showed up and started threatening Emersyn, demanding money that she thinks Emersyn stole from her ex-husband. The police were called and the woman arrested," explained Jaya.

A woman with a small child? He remembered noticing an attractive woman with a small child that morning. Could she have been the reason Emersyn had behaved so strangely? Arlo felt worse, if that were possible. "I have screwed this whole thing up," he told Jaya.

She didn't deny it.

"It would appear that I don't know as much about women as I thought."

Jaya laughed. "Oh, you have mastered the art of getting a woman, now you have to figure out how to keep the right one."

"It would appear to be more difficult than I first thought," admitted Arlo.

"Things that are worthwhile usually are."

"Arlo?" he heard his mother call. "Can you come and set the table please?"

"Jaya, I got to go set the table." He laughed.

"So I heard. I'll see you on Monday. And, Arlo, I'm glad your dad is okay."

"Thank you." Arlo hung up and went to set the table.

"Everything good?" his dad asked as he handed him cutlery and napkins.

"Yeah, just a lot of changes going on at work." Arlo set the table and tried to not think about returning to work in two days and not seeing Emersyn. Not finding excuses to walk by her office or watching her leave to have lunch with Jaya. He wondered if he had of taken the time to tell her where he was going and allowed her to explain what had happened in the lobby if she would have taken the job. Now he would never know.

◆

Emersyn

Harvey patted Emersyn's back as she cried into his crisp white shirt. Her weeping eventually settled and she sniffed and wiped her nose on her sleeve, earning her a disdainful look from her friend. He handed her a paper napkin from the picnic basket

"Are you sure you are okay with us moving to LA?" she asked for the fifth time that week. Emersyn had come home Monday night and announced that she had accepted a job in LA and that she would love it if Harvey would come with her. He had told her that he was happy to move, but everyday after that she had asked again. Emersyn was worried she was taking Harvey farther away from his daughters. They were a close-knit family and she didn't want to cause them any heartache.

"I am sure, Miss Emersyn. I am looking forward to letting my hair down on the open road for the next week."

Emersyn laughed. Harvey was completely bald. "It feels a bit like Deja vous. You heading off in my gorgeous car, while I get stuck on a plane and miss out on all the fun. I get to find the house and office space all while you are driving. Somehow that doesn't seem fair." She became serious. "But what about when we get there?"

"I've always wanted to see LA, this is my chance." He stood up and began to collect all the leftover foods and dishes from the impromptu picnic. "Besides, what would I do with myself if I didn't go with you? Garden? Find a hobby?" He smiled down at her. "I like taking care of you, Miss Emersyn, and I will continue to until you let me go."

"Thank you, Harvey. But you do know I'm never letting you go," said Emersyn.

"Suits me just fine." Harvey finished packing up and stood holding the rubbish bag in one hand and the picnic basket in the other. "Thank you for asking me on your picnic. Don't forget Miss Jaya will be here in an hour."

"I won't be long, just a couple more minutes and I'll do that final bit of packing."

"Very well."

Harvey left her under the large, glorious tree that her mother had chosen as her picnic spot in this house so many years ago. She stood and brushed off the grass that stuck to her jeans. "Miss you, Mom," she whispered as she placed her hand on the rough bark of the tree. Emersyn stood there for a few more minutes before saying her final good bye and heading upstairs to have a shower and get dressed to go to the airport.

As she showered, her thoughts wondered, and as always if she didn't guard them they ended up on Arlo. The same questions looped in her mind. Why had he left? Why hadn't he called? What had she done to deserve this behavior? And then there was the cycle of self-recriminations. Why had she fallen for him? Why had she really considered not going to LA when she didn't know him? Why, after all the pain with Nicolai, had she been stupid enough to trust a man? Especially a man like Arlo...

There were no answers to these questions and it was torture for her to go over them, but maybe this time she would learn and not fall for a beautiful face with pretty words and no heart again. It had opened old wounds and she was struggling to close them.

In some ways she was looking forward to LA. The challenges of starting from scratch, integrating a whole team, and being able to implement all her own ideas about the way her section should run without any interference or comparisons would be exciting. Jeremy had been thrilled to take on the chance of finding Emersyn somewhere to live in such a short amount of time. She was happy to stay in a hotel for a week or two, as the company was picking up the tab, but she wanted to settle down as soon as feasible.

Jaya arrived just as Emersyn was putting the final toiletries in her luggage. The rest would be packed and shipped, all supervised by Harvey in the next day or two, and then he would be on his way in her car.

"Thank you again for letting me live in your apartment while I'm in New York."

"No problem. It was standing empty, as it is usually rented out on a monthly or quarterly lease by the studios when they are filming in New York. There was nothing on the books, so I talked to Dad and he was happy to let you use it until you figure if you like New York enough to go permanent."

"You are a wonderful friend." Jaya sniffed.

"No crying. I can't leave if you cry." Emersyn grabbed both of Jaya's shoulders and gave her a shake. "This is supposed to be exciting times. We are off on big adventures."

Jaya laughed before her face took on a serious expression and she unconsciously flicked her long, dark braid over her shoulder. "I am so sorry about Arlo. I can't believe he just up and left everything without explanation."

Emersyn grimaced. They had rehashed this conversation too many times. "Arlo is not your responsibility." She changed the subject. "What I really want to know is will you be known in New York as Jaya Reynolds or Jaya Chatterjee. Who will I be asking for when I ring?"

"I took your advice and decided that it was a good chance for me to change my name without there being too many repercussions and confusion."

"Wonderful. I wish we had time for a drink to celebrate, but that will have to wait until we get time to visit." Emersyn grinned as Harvey waited in the doorway, having put her things in Jaya's car. "You come to me and we get Harvey to make more cocktails."

"Done." Jaya gave Harvey a quick hug as she walked out the house. "You take care of our girl, okay?"

"Always, Miss Jaya." He smiled fondly at her.

Emersyn embraced Harvey and kissed his cheek. "Drive safe, and I'll see you in a few weeks."

"Ring if you need anything, Miss Emersyn. I can still take care of you from a distance."

"Harvey, you are the best." She smiled as she climbed into Jaya's car.

—◆—

Ruby, Henry Tran's personal assistant, waved cheerfully as Jaya pulled up to the short term car park. A short, tubby man in his early forties, stood holding the hand of a chubby faced boy, aged around five. It didn't take long for Jaya and Emersyn to load up the cart Ruby had been keeping for her with the two large suitcases, garment bag, and matching make-up case that Emersyn was taking with her until the rest of her belongings arrived in a week or two.

Jaya embraced Emersyn firmly and whispered, "I am going to miss you."

Emersyn held her tightly. "I will miss you too." She kissed her cheek. "Now, no crying."

"Don't forget to have fun," said Jaya as she grinned at Emersyn. "I will talk to you in a few days. I am going to be picking your brain about New York."

"I look forward to it." Emersyn noted the security guard strolling toward them. They were probably over their allotted time in the car park. "Time for you to go."

"It looks like it." One more quick embrace and Jaya let her go. "Good luck with everything, Ruby." Jaya waved at the group as she climbed back in the car.

Emersyn turned the Ruby's family. "Hi, I'm Emersyn."

"This is my partner Jack, and our son, Toby." Ruby introduced them.

Jack shook Emersyn's hand. "It's great to meet you."

"You too." Emersyn kneeled down. "Hi, Toby."

The little boy smiled shyly and held out his hand. "Hi."

Emersyn took the small, cute hand and shook it. "I was thinking the company Christmas party should be at Disneyland this year. What do you think?"

Toby nodded his head so vigorously that all three adults laughed.

"We shall see what I can organize." Emersyn winked at him before she stood up and grabbed her cart. "I guess we should go."

As they moved to the entrance, Emersyn fought the urge to look around in the hope that Arlo was there, waiting to profess his love and tell her that they could make a long distance relationship work. Her heart ached for what could have been, but as she lined up behind Ruby's family, Emersyn resolutely straightened her shoulders and looked forward. *The future is the only place you don't feel pain. It is a place where you are healed and happy and free of regret. It is a place where lessons have been learned and will not be repeated.* Emersyn smiled as the man on the check-in counter beckoned to her. *The future is lonely,* a subdued voice told her.

Chapter 31

Emersyn

"Thanks for being so patient about this," Jeremy said for the third time as he opened the car door for Emersyn.

"It's fine. I gave you five days notice that I was moving out here. I knew it would take some time for you to find me the right place." Emersyn slid into the tan leather-passenger's seat of Jeremy's BMW and put her seat belt on.

"It's taken me a little longer than I thought it would, but the perfect house has just come onto the market. It's a bit bigger than you had originally requested, but the price is right and it's in a great neighbourhood. The commute to work will still be hell, but we're in LA so when isn't the commute to work hell?"

Emersyn settled further into her seat and enjoyed the warm morning sun coming through the sunroof as Jeremy pulled the car out into the traffic that streamed past her inner LA hotel 24 hours a day. As they headed toward a more affluent part of the city, she explained how the office set-up was complete and that they would officially start taking new clients on the Monday after New Year. Aside from interviewing staff and organizing the office set-up with Ruby, Emersyn had been helping Matilda, who had arrived from Austin a week ago. She came with her husband, John, and their three children to complete the organizing of the Happy Girl launch on New Year's Eve. Matilda had been doing the launch preparation from Austin prior, and had been planning on coming out just after Christmas to work with Pascal, the young woman who was the brains behind Happy Girl and their marketing team. Now with the opening of the Chalmers and Tran Advertising Agency in LA and Matilda accepting the transfer offer, she could be available for a more hands-on role for the final three weeks of preparation.

"It has been a challenge to push myself out of my accountant brain comfort zone, but I have learned so much more hands-on information about the company, what is needed, and what every role represents. We are starting out small and will add more staff as we grow."

"How many in total have come from the other offices?"

"Ten from Austin, and thirteen from New York. Most are middle or lower tier employees and put their hands up when it was announced that transfers to other offices could be an option."

"So you and the head of the marketing team were the only two higher placed ones that moved?"

"Henry Tran, as in Chalmers and Tran, has come from Austin with his PA, Ruby. The head of marketing in New York took the role here."

"How is that working out for you? A bit better than the last head of marketing you were dealing with in Austin?"

Emersyn hadn't told Jeremy what had happened with Arlo since their catch up the first night she had been in LA or about the Happy Girl bid. As far as he knew, Arlo was just a jerk who Emersyn had had to work with.

"Phil is great. Dedicated and hard working."

"Well, that sounds very boring." He knew her well. "What is the problem?"

Emersyn grimaced. "I hate to say it, but he is not Arlo." She sighed and looked out the car window as the iconic palm trees of the area sped by. "It's possible I'm being unfair, and I am willing to admit that I haven't seen him in action with any new clients, but he lacks something. Arlo has an energy when he works that I haven't seen in Phil yet."

"Mmmm." Jeremy was non-committal.

"I am waiting to see what he is like once we are open for business. I mean, he must be great or he wouldn't have done so well in New York, and they wouldn't have brought him out here if he wasn't up to it. Henry and Arthur are too business savvy to do anything to risk what they have built."

"Fair enough."

"Where are you taking me? I can't afford this area and to keep Harvey employed and my car running." Emersyn frowned as the feel of the place triggered a reminder of something.

Jeremy laughed as they continued their drive through the richer suburbs. "We are almost there, and trust me you can afford it."

They drove by high stone walls with massive metal security gates for several more minutes before Jeremy pulled into a driveway of a gray stone-walled property. There were gorgeous wrought iron gates that were large enough to be imposing on anyone that stood at the front of them. Jeremy pushed a button on the controller he had stored in the middle console of his car and the gates began to swing open. Emersyn's mind continued to fight through her memories to discover why the place felt familiar. They drove up the long driveway that was lined with palm trees and came to park in front of a sprawling mansion that was built in the same stone as the high walls that surrounded it. Wrought iron double doors, that too matched the outer gates, protected an entry hall with the house's official glass front doors within the security of the entry area.

"I have been here before," Emersyn announced.

"Yes." Jeremy took out a key and opened the gates before heading to the glass doors and unlocking those.

Emersyn followed him in, her feelings of Deja vu growing. The glass doors brought them into a wide hallway that had gold side tables with glass tops placed along the walls in between the open arched doorways, two doors stood on each side of the long hallway, with another wide entrance at the end. Each side table held a small, white decorated Christmas tree with gold baubles and tinsel, complete with tiny sparkling lights and a gold star on top of the tree. Above each thin side table was a large rectangular shaped mirror, with a heavy gold edge that reflected all the trees. The look was completed with a stark white marble floor. Very different from all the warm beiges and sweeping spiral staircase in the house in Austin. This house was cool and modern and stunning in its simplicity.

"That side is the entertaining section of the house." He waved his hand to the left. "This side is the more relaxed living area and study with a massive library. The back arch is where you will find the entrance to the bedrooms and kitchen, and a way out into the back area. But I think you should start with this room first." He indicated to his right. "The informal living area is wonderful."

"Lead the way then." Emersyn was thinking maybe she had been in the house at some point when they had lived in LA during her childhood. As she stepped through the large arched doorway, every-thing came back to her. This was her family home, and the proof still hung over the faux fireplace that dominated the large wall. A beautiful painting of a young woman with green eyes and auburn hair smiling down at her green-eyed daughter with pure love covered a large section of the wall. It was done in muted tones of white and gold with only the hair and eye color standing out. It was an extraordinary piece of art.

"That's you and your mom, isn't it?" asked Jeremy, breaking the spell the painting had placed on her.

"Yes—" Emersyn's voice caught and she had to clear her throat and say it again. "Yes."

"You look a bit like her, and now I know where your great eyes come from."

Emersyn sat down in the closest chair. "How?"

Jeremy looked a little uncomfortable as he took a seat in the large, brilliant white leather lounge across from her. "I knew you were coming to LA before you told me." His gaze remained on the painting, rather than looking at her.

"How is that possible?" She frowned for a moment. "No, don't answer it. I figured it out. Thomas rang you."

Jeremy looked relieved. "Yes, your dad rang me and made it very clear that if I wanted to keep his listings I needed to get you back into the family house. That there is nowhere else you should be living while in LA."

"Didn't you tell me the last time I was out here that this place had been leased for twelve months? That was only about five months ago." Emersyn narrowed her eyes at Jeremy. "Where are the people that were living here?"

"I purchased another place on behalf of your father and then moved them in there. He paid to have all their belongings packed and moved and gave them a month of free rent. It's only a few doors down, so it didn't inconvenience them too much. It just took a few weeks to get it all done."

"You did all that in just under five weeks?"

"I am good at my job." Jeremy looked at her, his brown eyes earnest. "Please tell me you will stay after all the effort I went to on behalf of your father to get you here? And I told you you could afford it."

Emersyn couldn't help herself, and she nodded. She knew she should be angry at being manipulated, but this is all her father was capable of giving her. Beautiful, expensive homes to live in for free. It was impossible for him to move on from her mother's death and be a parent to her, so he made sure she was provided for instead. The bright winter sun poured through the large, arched picture windows and warmed Emersyn's back as she looked around the room, her eyes finally coming to rest on the large white undecorated Christmas tree standing in the far corner. Several boxes stood next to the tree, and she got up to see what was inside.

"Your father told me to set up the tree and bring in the boxes that were in storage out in the garage," Jeremy explained.

"You set up the Christmas tree?" Emersyn was surprised.

"Ahhh, no. I don't even have one myself. I just got a couple of the sign guys to come out and do it."

"Well, in that case, for payback you can join me and a girlfriend that is flying in in two days with helping us decorate it. I think that is only fair."

"Do I have any choice?"

"No. Now let's see the rest of the house. I am assuming all my belongings were shipped here and aren't in storage like I thought they were?"

Jeremy managed to look sheepish yet innocent at the same time.

⁕

Arlo

The restaurant was busy, and the noise was bothering Arlo. The crowded French eatery was one of his several go-to places for dates, but he hadn't been out on a date for a few months, having made the decision to stop mindlessly dating a month before his fateful weekend with Emersyn. But now she had been gone a month and there was very little chance he could see of fixing the current situation, so he had allowed his friend Ray to set him up on a date with one of his colleagues from work. Ray had never fixed him up before, admitting that Arlo's womanizing ways was not something he would subject his female friends to. Arlo had been a little ashamed to discover Ray had felt that way about his dating habits. Arlo had always felt that by being open with the women he went out with, by explaining to them he didn't want any commitment or attachment, would make everything fine He was now aware of how unfair he had been and how a few of those women had ended up hurt by him, even though it was unintentional.

But now Emersyn was gone, having taken a transfer to the new LA office, and Arlo was left to wonder how it had all gone wrong so quickly after they had both let their guards down to be together. If he was honest, a major lack of communication on his behalf had certainly contributed to the problem, and his leaving the situation on two occasions when he should have stayed and talked to her had compounded the whole mess. Arlo had moped around the office for the first two weeks she had left and then his second in charge, Jaya, had transferred to the New York office two weeks ago and he had felt completely out of sorts. That was when Ray had suggested there was a girl at work that Arlo might be interested in having dinner with.

Arlo fought to bring his concentration back to the woman who sat across from him. The conversation had started out well enough with them discovering they both enjoyed watching basketball and baseball, and having a spirited argument regarding who the better teams were. That had lasted until the main meal had been served and Arlo had asked her a few questions about her personal life, where she had launched into antidote after antidote of the whimsical and funny things her four-year-old daughter did that only a parent would find amusing. He had smiled and murmured several encouraging words, but the meal was finished and yet she still had more tales to tell and now photos on the phone had come out too. She was an attractive woman and six months ago he would have considered sleeping her, but now it didn't interest him. The waiter offered them dessert and he was grateful when she declined. They finished their drinks, she offered to pay for her dinner, but he paid for both of them and told her he had a great time and saw her into an Uber.

As he walked the hundred metres to his car, Arlo couldn't believe how much his thinking had changed and how he looked forward to going home. It didn't take him long to reach his apartment, and the first thing he did was take a shower and let the water run over him. He found his mind wandering and in the steam that formed on the glass shower screen he drew a love heart and put his initials in it just like Emersyn had described teenage girls doing. His hand paused as his heart constricted before he followed through with adding E.C in the bottom section of the heart. He let the heart sit there, slowly losing its form as more steam built over the top of it.

He missed her. He missed her emerald eyes and the burgundy hair that had covered him as they had been in her bed and she had leaned to kiss him. He missed her demanding ways at work, pushing him to always perform to the best of himself. And he missed the way a little line appeared between her eyes as her thoughts grew intense when she spoke about things that had great importance to her. He had not realised how much time he had spent studying her until she was gone and he had ruined any chance of being together.

Arlo turned off the shower and put on a t-shirt and loose track pants. He flicked on the TV and turned on the kettle as he grabbed his laptop and a folder filled with information and ideas he had jotted down regarding the most important campaign he would have the chance to pitch just after New Year. He considered ringing Jaya and asking her thoughts on a few things as she had always made an excellent sounding board, but he knew ethically he should be ringing his new second-in-charge, Bryce, about his opinions. Bryce had turned out to be a middle-aged man with a great sense of humor that Arlo got along well with, but he lacked Jaya's ability to create her own ideas. He was a great second in charge, able to work with all the team members, and oversee tasks and encourage where needed. But he would never be the head of marketing as he just didn't have the overall creative abilities required.

Instead of ringing Jaya, he texted Ray.

A: Hey, back from the date.

Ray must have been sitting with his phone in his hand as the response was almost instantaneous.

R: How was it? Isn't she great? I thought you would have lots in common.

A: You forgot to mention she had a daughter.

R: I did?

A: Very funny.

R: So?????

A: She was nice, but not really my type.

R: Why?

A: Once we exhausted talking sports, all she talked about was the kid - with photos too.

R: Oh shit. Sorry. Didn't think she would do that.

A: Yeah, I think I will give anymore of your choices a miss.

R: Okay. I won't interfere again. You going home for Christmas? Or do you want to come to our place like Thanksgiving?

A: Thanks for the offer, I did enjoy spending the holiday with you, but my folks are expecting me home for Christmas. After Dad's cancer scare, I really want to go spend more time with them.

R: No problem. Talk soon.

Arlo put the phone down, picked up the tv remote, and began to click through the channels. He stopped as a familiar face filled the screen. Felicity, a woman he dated for several months when Emersyn had just arrived in Austin was reporting at a local theatre event. Her goal had been to graduate from weather girl on a local morning show to become their entertainment reporter. Two weeks ago that had become a reality and Arlo was very much looking forward to being her first in studio interview on Monday morning.

Chapter 32

Arlo

Arlo sat stiffly in the make-up chair as the friendly team of stylists applied the final touches to his dark, wavy hair. He had brought in several shirts to wear with his charc beenoal-colored trousers and the stylists' had chosen a soft, sage-green button shirt. After all the shine was removed from his face, Arlo was ushered to the green room, where several other guests for that mornings show were waiting to film their interview or segment. There was a celebrity chef and the members of a popular country band, plus an animal ranger of some kind. She had a covered cage sitting on the floor at her feet, and Arlo was curious to find out what it was. He went to sit next to her, but she was called away as he sat down.

As he waited, he took out his phone and quickly sent a message to his email as a reminder of an idea he had just had, and then made sure it was on silent and not vibrate. He sat in his seat and watched the park ranger on the monitor as she brought out a Bobcat cub from the covered cage. Her enthusiasm was contagious, and he found himself grinning as the anchor attempted to hold the animal in the way he had been instructed and it urinated on his lap. The ranger's face had been relaxed and quite cheerful when she explained that it was an occupational hazard.

"Five minutes," a stylist with a headset walked in and announced while looking at him. Arlo stood and his protective cape was whisked off, and he was escorted out of the room and onto the studio floor, where the microphone that had been attached to his collar was adjusted and the battery pack clipped to the back of his belt was turned on. Arlo was walked silently to a comfortable-looking, cream upholstered chair and indicated to sit while Felicity sat opposite him, having her own mic adjusted. He hadn't had the opportunity to chat with Felicity before the beginning of the segment so the first time he would speak to her since they had stopped sleeping together was going to be on live television. He hoped that she had been as okay when he had stopped seeing her as she had appeared to be.

She smiled at him through all the people between them and winked. All the anxiety he felt slipped away as he realized she was just as fun and genuine as he remembered. Arlo returned the smile and wink just as everyone around them cleared the floor.

"And Felicity has a guest, live in the studio today," the morning anchor announced.

Both Arlo and Felicity smiled at the camera and Arlo relaxed as presenting was his thing. This was no different to standing in a conference room pitching to an important client and he thrived in that environment.

"Thank you, Steve. Today I'd like to introduce you to the very talented Arlo Medina, the Head of Marketing at Chalmers and Tran Advertising Agency here in Austin. And I bet you are all wondering why the new entertainment reporter is speaking to him?" Felicity paused for effect and smiled cheekily at the camera. "Well, Arlo has a ticket to the hottest party on New Year's Eve, and I thought we should talk about it." She turned to him and smiled, inviting him to speak.

"Thank you for allowing me to come on and talk about the latest Happy Girl launch."

"Can you give us a bit of background to Happy Girl and how you fit into this? As I understand, they are based in LA and yet a firm from Austin is running the campaign."

"Happy Girl is the brainchild of Tiffany Bowen, and with the backing of her supportive father, Michael, has become one of the major players in the teen market for cosmetics and skin care. Tiffany is currently completing her degree in marketing and will take over all marketing of the brand once she graduates. Chalmers and Tran were brought in specifically for this new product range and are excited to see it through, which is why I am here with you today."

Felicity leaned forward, looking interested in every word he spoke. "Can you give us any hints on what the new product line will be?"

Arlo leaned in as if he were going to share a secret and smiled charmingly at her. He was enjoying himself. "No."

This brought a pout to the pretty features of the new entertainment reporter.

"You have to be at the party to see the launch and the ads begin New Year's Day, because we should all start the new year looking our best."

"When does this exciting new product hit the stores?"

"New Year's Day. Everything will be available immediately. After all, you can only postpone gratification for so long and we have made you wait for months now."

Felicity laughed lightly and settled back into her seat. "We are running out of time, but I still have a few more questions for you."

"Go ahead." Arlo also moved back in his chair.

"Why aren't you in LA helping with the finishing touches to the launch? I have heard that Chalmers and Tran have opened an office out there."

"Our events coordinator from Austin has moved out there and is working in conjunction with the Happy Girl team to make it the perfect party. I am working on some exciting new things that I will be happy to come back and talk to you about at another time. Maybe we can get you into one of those party launches?" He smiled at her and wanted to wink but knew that would look bad on camera. He wanted to appear friendly, but not flirtatious.

Felicity laughed. "I look forward to it. You are welcome to come back anytime."

"Thanks."

"Our time is up, but I want to take the opportunity to wish you a very Merry Christmas and every success with the Happy Girl launch. I look forward to the pictures that will no doubt be uploaded everywhere."

Arlo smiled at her and then at the camera with the red light above it. "Thank you for having me, and from Chalmers and Tran in Austin, New York, and now LA, we wish everyone a wonderful and safe Christmas."

They all sat there for several seconds before it was announced they had gone to an ad break, and everyone began to move at once. Mics were unhooked, sets were moved, and Arlo was led by Felicity off the sound stage and out into the overcast, early morning. As soon as they were outside, she grabbed and hugged him. "It is so great to see you. You were fabulous."

He returned the hug. "Thank you for doing that at such short notice. You definitely appear to have got the hang of interviewing down. I felt relaxed and your questions were interesting."

"I want to report on more than just the latest basic entertainment stuff and further afield than our own state, so it was perfect. They keep saying they want to widen the demographic of our viewers and I think talking about the major launch of Happy Girl certainly is a demographic. And I got to help a friend out."

"How have you been?" he asked her.

"Great. I have started seeing a new guy. He works on the show, so understands the crazy hours I work. And like you, he doesn't see me as just a weather girl."

"That is fantastic. What are your Christmas plans?"

Felicity's face soured for a moment. "I am going to stay in the city with him. Divorced parents are being painful so I am skipping the lot. There is always plenty to report around Christmas time, so I am happy to stay and work. What about you?"

"I'm flying home for Christmas tonight and then will fly from there to LA on the 30th for the launch."

"Busy boy. How many girls you dating at the moment?" she asked impishly.

"None. Dating and I have parted ways for a while."

Felicity's blue eyes narrowed, and a slow smile spread across her fine features. "Who's the girl? The same one you stopped seeing me for?"

"There is no girl."

"I don't believe you, but if that is what you want to tell yourself we will go with it."

"Good, because that is what I am telling myself at the moment," Arlo admitted.

Someone stuck their head out of the door they stood next to. "Felicity, fifteen minutes."

"Thanks. I'll be right in." She turned to Arlo. "I gotta go. Time to go introduce the band."

"I saw them in the green room."

She gave him another hug. "I hope everything goes well with the launch and the girl."

Chapter 33

Emersyn

The kettle had just begun to boil when she flicked it off, hoping not to wake Harvey as it was only 5:45 a.m. Emersyn rubbed her gritty-feeling eyes as she waited for the tea bag to steep and stood quietly, her knee length, ratty old cardigan wrapped tightly around her. The stark white kitchen, with its expensive gold trimming and frosted glass cupboards didn't have the same appeal for her as the one in Austin with its blue and white tiles, breakfast nook, and large wooden table that she had left behind did. She pulled the cardigan tighter. It was definitely colder at night in LA, and Emersyn hadn't realised how quickly she had acclimatised to the heat until now. She completed making the cup of tea and made her way back to her beautiful bedroom, where she flicked on the television, and connected it to the internet to find the correct station through a streaming platform.

Emersyn rearranged the over-sized square pillows so she could sit propped up and climbed back into bed, pulling the plush duvet up to her chin and sipping her cup of tea. She watched as a friendly park ranger brought out a Bobcat from its cage and laughed as it peed all over the host of the morning show. During the ad break she checked her emails and calendar for the day and set a reminder for herself to pick up Jaya from the airport early the next morning. She finished her cup of tea and waited for the show to come back on.

The anchor from the morning show threw the interview over to Felicity, and without warning, Arlo's handsome features filled Emersyn's television screen. Her heart pounded and her breathing changed as she took in his strong brow and wavy, dark brown, short hair that she had run her fingers through. As he spoke, her mind recoiled and fought to suppress the sound of sweet nothings he had whispered in her ear as he entered her and brought her to climax. Emersyn's reactions were unexpected as she had been keeping a tight lid on her thoughts about him.

She watched with growing confusion as her want for his sweet lips and direct questions warred with her anger and resentment as he flirted with the perfectly pretty host of the segment. He laughed conspiratorially with her when he had leaned in to answer a question, only for him to be coy and avoid the question. His innuendo was clever but not overly done, but it felt like a kick in the gut to Emersyn.

Arlo was a natural in the interview and his answers would reflect well for Chalmers and Tran as well as Happy Girl. Like many things he did in the industry, it was a stroke of genius to talk about the launch as the place to be on New Year's Eve. She wondered how he had managed to get a booking on the most popular morning show in Texas so quickly. Emersyn watched as the two wrapped up the segment and suddenly remembered he had been dating a weather girl somewhere along the way. Could it be the same channel? Without thought of the repercussions to her heart, she pulled up the website for the show and discovered that the weather girl, Felicity, had now become their entertainment reporter and that they were wanting to change direction by reporting a slew of interesting things going on not just in their state. The show went to an ad break and Emersyn got up and turned it off as she headed toward her bathroom.

That's why they were so friendly and relaxed together, she thought as she threw her sleeping gear in the hidden hamper and turned the shower on. *You only get that sort of rapport once you have been intimate.* Emersyn stepped down the two steps and into the sunken, walk-in shower, with its half wall and no shower screen. She had been happy to discover her bathroom had no glass shower screen as they now reminded her of Arlo and she needed no more reminders. *They could have reigned the flirting in a little; it was tad unprofessional*, she thought as she wet her hair and grabbed the shampoo.

Emersyn spent the remainder of her morning preparations dissecting the interview. She knew it wasn't healthy, but it was like an insect bite you shouldn't scratch but did it anyway. It was nice to be distracted with these feelings, rather than the ones she had been dealing with since he had disappeared to his parents' and she had taken the job in LA. He had played her well and she was mortified that after swearing to never allow another man in to hurt her, she had done exactly that. But the worst thing was she had done it on purpose. Emersyn had kept him at bay for months when his intentions became clear. It had all come to a point where she couldn't decide how she had felt and thought it would be a splendid idea to sleep with him to get him out of her system. That had been a complete disaster. Instead, it had got her out of his system, as he couldn't wait to get away from her, twice, while she had fallen in love with him.

Now I am alone in LA with Harvey and a wounded heart. You are an idiot.

She put the final touches to her bun and made her way downstairs to where Harvey would have her breakfast waiting—the only dependable man in her life and who had her back, even though she paid him to work for her.

Emersyn

It had been a good day, despite the morning of self-recriminations and loathing for the flirting she had witnessed, Emersyn had managed to move passed it and get a lot of work completed. She flopped down in her gorgeous, soft upholstered chair and looked out her office window, pulling out the sushi rolls she had picked up on her way back to the office after a fruitful interview for what she felt could be her new second in charge.

As she ate the tuna roll, she thought about tomorrow and couldn't contain her excitement. Jaya flew in early in the morning and then they were off to the office Christmas Party at Disneyland, just as Emersyn had promised Ruby's son at the airport when they had flown to LA together. When Emersyn had floated the idea to Henry Tran, when he had arrived to take over as CEO of the LA branch, he had thought it wonderful and was happy to allow everyone a day off to attend. It did, of course, help that the office was still not technically open for business and they only had a small staff until they got more clients. Though it seemed, through the wonders of social media, word had got out about Arlo's interview and talk was growing about the Happy Girl launch as the LA office was taking phone calls from people interested in making appointments to discuss hiring them in the new year.

Emersyn had to silently congratulate Arlo to the fact his little performance that morning had done wonders for all three offices of Chalmers and Tran. He was slowly clawing back the respect he had lost after jeopardising the whole Happy Girl deal. She refused to dwell on that, and instead got her laptop and handbag to get her phone as her calendar was on that and she was enjoying sitting in her comfy chair rather than behind her desk.

Slowly she moved things around in her bag as she searched for the phone, muttering to herself that it had to be in there. She frowned and then decided it would be easier if she just took stuff out, instead of moving it around. Emersyn laid out the large wallet, sunglasses, car keys, small pencil case and slender writing pad—for those times where she needed to jot things down—and a small make-up bag on the low coffee table. Her phone was not in her bag. Now she stood and went to her jacket, which she had hung up behind her door to check the pockets. The phone was not in there. *SHIT.*

She opened the frosted glass office door to the outer office, where her PA sat. "Pedro, can you please ring down to the lobby and see if anyone has handed in a phone? I seem to have misplaced mine. Thanks."

"Sure. What type of phone? Any cover on it?"

Emersyn gave him the details and left the door open as she went back into the office and checked the floor, under her desk, down the side of her chair, and anywhere else she could think of that it might have slid down. She heard Pedro on the phone to the front desk of the office building. Finally, she gave up looking and put all her belongings back in her bag.

Pedro politely tapped on the open door. "There has been nothing handed in, but they have taken a note, in case someone does hand it in."

"Bugger. Okay, thank you."

"If you give me your keys, I can go check the car for you. You have that zoom meeting with the Austin office scheduled that you can't miss."

Emersyn dug back into her bag and took out the keys, which she tossed to him. "You are amazing. Thank you."

"No problem at all."

Pedro left the office and Emersyn flipped open her laptop and boot-ed it up. Cursing at herself for being paranoid and not turning on the find my phone function when she had got the phone. She played her day out in her head, trying to remember the last place she had used the phone in the hope she could backtrack. Now she thought about it, it could be in several places. While she waited for the meeting to start, she jotted down all the places she had been to since leaving the office earlier in the day.

Her zoom meeting with the new head of accounting in the Austin office took longer than expected as he was having trouble with the system she had in place, and he was only very new to managing people. He needed a bit more hand-holding and if she hadn't of run out of the Austin office with such haste he would have got it. Emersyn felt guilty about it, so checked in every few days to make sure he was coping and gave him tips on how to deal with people.

Once the meeting was concluded, Pedro came in and handed back her keys. "No luck."

"Thanks for looking." She pushed the notes she had taken earlier to him. "These are all the places I have been today. Could you possibly ring them and see if anyone has handed in a phone?"

He took the note. "Sure thing."

"Thanks." Emersyn went back to her desk chair and sat down heav-ily. She eventually went back to work as there was nothing she could do about the phone while Pedro was still attempting to track it down. His voice could be heard in the next office as he explained the situation several times.

By the end of the hour, the phone had not been located, and Emersyn had resigned herself to the fact she probably wasn't going to get it back. Though it was extremely inconvenient, she also looked at the bright side. Now her ex-husband and the woman he cheated on her with—and shared a daughter with—would no longer be able to contact her. "Can you please set up a new phone and number and then email out to the other offices so that everyone is aware I have a new number?"

Thank goodness for other forms of communication, she thought as she quickly messaged Jeremy, Jaya, and her father via MSN to explain what had happened.

Chapter 34

Emersyn

Santa 'ho ho'd' at the gathered children from Chalmers and Tran, and patted his knee for the first child to come and sit. Emersyn smiled happily and linked her arm with Jaya's as they looked on while the gifts were handed to each child. Emersyn had worked hard with the people at Disneyland to make sure each child had exactly what their parents had ticked on the wish list that had been emailed to them the fortnight prior. Everything went smoothly and with a heartwarmingly cute "thank you," uttered from a little boy dressed as Simba, they were all ushered into a large dining room, where they were greeted by Storm Troopers and Mulan at the door and were served by the boys of Neverland inside.

"I'll say it again. You, Emersyn, should have been an event coordinator," Matilda announced as she watched her own children squeal with glee as they interacted with the Storm Troopers. "This whole day has been perfect."

"Oh, I didn't do much." Emersyn brushed off the compliment. "I just told the event people here what I wanted, and they did the rest."

Matilda tilted back her head and laughed. "Ah, yes, that's what we do," she said in her Australian accent.

Everyone joined in the laughter as the children continued to play with the Disney characters present.

"What's next on the agenda?" Jaya asked.

"Family photos, but with a twist."

"Do tell?"

"Well, the adults or teens over fourteen can't wear costumes in the park, but I have organized for us to have full access to the shops, and we can all get dressed up as our favourite character and have photos taken. You can all go for a family themed dress up or just your favourite character."

As everyone started discussing what they wanted to wear, Emersyn waved her hands to get their attention. "My only request is that you don't take off your costume until everyone is dressed and we can have a company photo."

The young woman that had been on hand for all their needs for the day stood up to get their attention. "If one of the families has finished eating, I can take you down to the costume and photography area so we can get started. This can take a bit of time, so please be patient."

"Wow. I love you, Emersyn." Jaya grinned at her. "Do you have any idea how much I want to be a Disney Princess?"

"Now, you just have to figure out which one."

"Oh, too easy. I love the movie *Tangled*. A photo of me as Rapunzel, holding a frying pan, will be just perfect. What about you?"

Emersyn flushed. "I was so busy organising everything that I hadn't really thought about it. And I am a little out of the loop as I never see Disney movies anymore."

They spent the next fifteen minutes discussing Disney Princesses and who was classed as one now Disney had bought out several studios. "I think I will be Merida from Brave. She didn't need a Prince Charming and neither do I."

Jaya gave her a knowing look but didn't say anything in front of the other people.

It took over an hour but finally everyone was dressed and all family photos had been snapped. Now the collective families of Chalmers and Tran Advertising Agency in the newly established LA office gathered to have their photo taken. Once that was done, all the children were taken out of the photo and kept entertained by Mulan and Jaya-Rapunzel as the staff had their first photo taken as a team. There was much giggling and a bit of role playing throughout the photo shoot.

Once finished and all back into their normal clothing, Emersyn thanked everyone for coming and handed over speeches to Henry Tran. He wished everyone a Merry Christmas and told them that he didn't expect to see anyone in the office until the day after Boxing Day and to enjoy their break, because he planned on making them work hard once they returned. There was cheering at the news that they had several days off, and Emersyn told them they were free to leave or stay at the park, and their time was now their own. But whomever stayed there for the remainder of the day, there would be a Christmas Fantasy Parade at the end of the night and she and Jaya would be attending if anyone wanted to join them.

The families with small children said their farewells, while others went off to explore the park some more. Emersyn found herself a part of a group of seven, all the single people from the agency had gathered to continue the fun together. They spent the remainder of the day enjoying the rides and other attractions and it all ended with a large group of them, as several of the families had stayed to all watch the parade together. Emersyn had found the day to be magical in every way and was happy and exhausted as she and Jaya climbed into her car and started the drive home.

Emerysn

Jaya took a sip of the cocktail Harvey had whipped up and sighed with contentment. "Oh, how I have missed you and your bartending skills."

"Don't get used to them; he flies out tomorrow to spend Christmas with his girls and their families," Emersyn warned her.

"Oh, that isn't very fair. I just got here." Jaya pouted at the both of them.

"Never fear, Miss Jaya, I shall be back a few days before you go home. It's a quick visit as they all have to go back to work and school," Harvey explained.

Jaya took another sip and studied him. Emersyn wondered what she was thinking. "Why do you make him wear that crazy butler outfit, Emmy?"

Emersyn groaned as if it was painful. "When he worked for Nicolai he was expected to wear the fancy uniform. When I left and Harvey came with me, I told him he needn't wear it any longer, but he stubbornly refuses."

"So, why do you wear it, Harvey?"

"I am a butler, Miss Jaya. My uniform tells people who come to the house or see me out with Miss Emersyn very clearly what I am."

"True, but are you not more?" Jaya pushed. "Are you not her friend, someone she relies on and trusts, when she trusts so few?"

Harvey stirred the contents of a glass jug, adding ice and mint leaves. "Yes. I am all those things, and wearing a uniform won't change that."

"Jaya, let it go. You can't win this one. I have been trying for over a year." Emersyn stood up and turned the portable speaker on that she had set up.

The interrogation of Harvey by Jaya continued. "How have you not been snapped up, Harvey?"

"Miss Emersyn needs me."

"So you both hide in her very fancy mansion." Jaya stared at them both pointedly.

Emersyn scrolled through the music on her phone and ignored the question. Harvey continued to stir his cocktail.

Jaya changed tack. "Harvey, will you be joining us for the Happy Girl launch on New Year's Eve?"

"I don't know. Miss Emersyn mentioned it, but I have not committed."

"Are you waiting for a better offer?"

Harvey's heavy lined, middle-aged face broke into a smile. "No."

"Excellent. It is settled then. You will be mine and Emmy's New Year's Eve date as I don't have one, and let's face it, Emersyn won't have one."

Harvey didn't answer instead he looked to Emersyn. "First off, I want you to know that I would have had a date, but my friend Jeremy already had plans before I arrived." Jaya raised her eyebrows but didn't comment. "Secondly, I think it is a great idea, but with one condition."

Both Jaya and Harvey looked suspicious as they waited for her condition.

"No uniform."

Jaya clapped her hands and laughed. "Yes, no uniform."

With the music playing, Emersyn lay back down on her sun lounge. "How did the name change go?"

"More smoothly than I had anticipated." Jaya raised her glass at Emersyn. "Thank you for the encouragement to do it. I feel like I have reclaimed me."

"It makes me so happy to hear that. Are you enjoying New York?"

"I love it. The fast pace, and the people everywhere. I think I was born to live in New York. I am trying every pretzel place I come across to see which is the best one. I may put on a few pounds before I find it, but it will be so worth it." Jaya patted her already plump tummy. "I cannot thank you enough for the use of the apartment. The view is freakin' amazing. Why did you ever want to move away?"

"College was away from Dad and the memories, which meant away from New York." Emersyn didn't like to talk about her father and their very fragile relationship so changed the subject. "How is the office? Is the new guy settling in and listening to you?"

"Oh, he is an intelligent, polite, team player who works very hard to get the most out of everyone, but..." She let the response go unfinished.

Emersyn completed it for her. "He is not Arlo. Matilda feels the same way here." She refused to include herself in the answer, even though she felt it too.

Harvey poured more drinks and went to turn the BBQ on before heading into the house to get what he needed.

Jaya hummed to the last few bars of the music. "How many questions you going to ask me before you get to the one you want to actually know about?"

"Hey, that's not fair. I want to know about everything you have been up to. I miss you and our lunch dates and Friday nights out partying," Emersyn defended herself.

"Okay, I am sorry. I miss you too. Heaps!" Jaya looked apologetic. "I was expecting you to ask me as soon as you saw me."

Emersyn looked out over the landscaped garden and her eyes came to rest on the glorious gazebo that was covered by vines that her mother had created adventurous picnics in. Reading her books and having tea parties. It brought her comfort to see it there. "I saw him on the morning show interview the other day and I didn't cope very well. He looked happy to be sitting there flirting with Felicity." Emersyn looked to Jaya and tried to keep the sadness from her voice. "I don't think I want to know the answer to how he is."

"You are going to have to deal with it soon. You do remember he will be here for New Year's Eve?"

Emersyn had been avoiding thinking about that.

Chapter 35

Arlo

Arlo frowned as he pressed the screen to end the call. Again, Emersyn had not answered her phone. Had she blocked him? It did not bode well for her ever forgiving him. Arlo had spent the Christmas break with his family and it had been wonderful. His father was recovering from his surgery and Arlo had forgotten just how much he enjoyed being with his niece and nephew, he vowed to make more of an effort to visit. Dating every weekend just didn't seem as appealing as spending time with family. This was the fifth time he had tried to call Emersyn on the pretence of wishing her a Merry Christmas, but the call just rang out each time. He wanted to talk to her, to hear her laugh, or berate him; he didn't care, he just needed to hear her. She consumed his thoughts and Arlo had been hoping to speak to her before the Happy Girl launch, but it was New Year's Eve tomorrow and she would not answer her phone.

He returned to packing his suitcase; he had to leave in an hour and he had put his packing off till the last minute. There was a polite tap on his open door. "You need anything?" his father asked as he walked into the room carrying several pairs of pressed trousers Arlo's mother had just ironed for him.

"Can you make a girl return my calls?" Arlo joked as he took the pants and put them in his suitcase.

Louis raised his eyebrows at his son. "You want a girl to return your calls? Where have you put my son?"

"Yeah, I know. It surprised me too. But I did something really dumb, and she won't talk to me."

"Do you know what you want?" his father asked his face serious. "Don't mess with her if you aren't certain."

"Yes." Arlo didn't hesitate, though he was surprised by how firm his father's voice was.

"Then why do I get the feeling you are holding back?"

"I'm not," Arlo said. Though now the words were out, maybe he was?

Louis sat down on the end of Arlo's bed. "If you really wanted to talk to this girl, I am certain you would find a way."

Arlo paused. His Papa was right. If Arlo truly wanted to force the issue, he could ring Jaya who he knew was currently staying with Emersyn. There was something holding him from doing more than calling her. He frowned as he pulled another shirt off its hanger and folded it neatly before placing it in the suitcase. "You might be right," he finally admitted.

"Might be?" scoffed Louis.

That made Arlo laugh. "Okay, you are right."

"Then I ask again, what is holding you back?"

"What if I really commit and she hurts me?" The words came out in a rush.

"Then you can say that for a while someone loved and cherished you and it was perfect."

Arlo stopped packing and looked to his father. "I have never felt this way before. She makes me want to be better. I want to make the world right for her. There is so much I don't know about her past, but

I know she has been through so much tragedy, and I think I just made it worse.”

“Then you must find the courage to lay your soul bare, give yourself to her, and accept all that she is.”

Arlo snorted as he took another shirt from a hanger. “You make it sound so easy.”

“Love is the easy bit. Trusting is the difficult part. Being open and vulnerable and giving another person yourself is scary.”

“I have never done that. I am not sure I can.” Arlo was brutally honest.

Louis stood and grasped his son’s shoulder. “It’s time to stop running.”

“Papa.” Arlo looked at his father seriously. “Sometimes I am not even sure what I am running from.”

“The unknown.”

“The unknown? What do you mean?”

“Ever since you were a boy you didn’t like messy. You like control; it’s safe and predictable. Emotions are messy, so you play the game, control the situation, and tell women exactly what to expect from you. As soon as someone stepped outside your control you moved on.”

Arlo blinked at him. He was right. How had he never seen it like that?

“This woman you haven’t been able to control the situation from the moment you met her is my guess?”

“Yes, I had to answer to her. She was in total control all the time.” Unbidden thoughts rose of Emersyn softening beneath his touch, willingly giving herself to him. Asking him to stay while in the kitchen the morning he had found out about the job offer. She had opened up to him, not a lot, but more than he had to her and what had he done? He had acted like a spoiled child who hadn’t been invited to a party because of his own behavior and had pushed her away. "Emmy showed me hints of who she was under the control."

"Emmy?"

"Emersyn."

"The woman you went to LA with?"

"You remembered that?" Arlo was surprised.

"Your mother and I both agreed that when you spoke about her you sounded different. We couldn't quite put our finger on it, but obviously now I know why."

"Why?"

"Because you love her. I think even back then your feelings ran deeper than you care to admit."

Arlo looked at the man who had moved countries to be with the woman he loved, his face earnest, waiting for his son to deny the words that now hung in the air. He couldn't. "I do love her," Arlo admitted. "I love her, and it terrifies me."

Louis nodded. "Yes. Be honest with her about it and whatever you did to make her not answer your calls. Own it."

Arlo remembered Emersyn's reaction when he was honest with her about himself and how she accepted him so willingly. He wanted her to be honest with him, but that wasn't going to happen until he shows her he is trustworthy and won't hurt her. His father was right. Arlo had come so far by letting go of what he thought a relationship should look like, but he wasn't being honest with himself or Emersyn. It was time to admit his faults and let go of his fear. Of course, it was far easier to say then do.

Chapter 36

Bubbles filled the entrance to the Happy Girl New Year's Eve launch party. Two large machines sat on either side of an arch that covered the double doorway, giving the impression you were walking into a large shower. Clear round balloons of varying sizes hanging from the ceiling to look like bubbles. A large fountain sat in the center of the room, spilling expensive bright pink punch into a marble bathtub filled with fruit. One wall was filled with bathroom mirrors that looked to be covered in steam and had a love heart with a Happy Girl product in the center of them. This reflected the ad campaign that would launch tomorrow. Under the mirrors were bathroom cabinets labelled with different hair types. Models with their hair wrapped in towels and wearing fluffy white and bubble gum pink bath robes with matching cute slippers stood next to the mirrors, handing out special sample bags of the different products.

On the other side of the room sat several pretend walk-in showers, also with the steamed effect and love hearts on the fake screens. Though they were actually photo booths, where you could fit two to six people inside at once. Behind the built-in camera was a wall of fun and frivolous things to wear. Top hats, headbands with love hearts sticking up, huge funky sunglasses, feather boas, all in the colors of the Happy Girl brand.

At the back of the room was a raised stage where a five-piece band would help them see in the new year. In front of the stage was a square, neon, flashing pink dance floor that felt like a throwback to the discos of the 70's. The band were doing their final sound check as Emersyn walked in, escorted by Harvey and Jaya. The first guests were expected to arrive in thirty minutes, and according to Matilda, who had been there supervising the set-up for the afternoon, everything was on schedule.

"What do you think?" Matilda asked as she came to stand next to Emersyn, an old-fashioned clipboard in her hand.

"I think it looks amazing," Emersyn answered with clear enthusiasm. "You have outdone yourself."

Matilda smiled warmly. "Thank you, but I still say you are in the wrong profession. You would make an excellent event coordinator. You have a true eye for styling."

"I get it from my mom." Emersyn said it quietly, accepting the compliment.

"Oh, my freakin god—" Their conversation was interrupted by a loud voice. Everyone turned to see the brains behind the Happy Girl brand standing still at the entrance of the room, bubbles falling around her. "I leave for a mere two hours to get my hair and make-up done and return to this transformation. You guys truly are the best in the business," Tiffany announced as she walked into the room. Michael, her father, followed after her.

Tiffany wore a silver dress that barely covered her butt and boobs. It was metallic, as if covered in mirrors, and had a single shoulder neckline with an asymmetrical hemline that came down to a point on the opposite side, mid-thigh. Her usual blonde hair was now covered in a wig of bubble gum pink, ultra long hair that was pulled up into a tight, slick ponytail. She teetered on clear high heels. She was spectacular to look at, and what would have looked ridiculous on most, looked stunning on her. Michael wore a perfectly cut black suit with a stiff white shirt, but to match his daughter he had a bright pink tie with a silver pin and matching cuffs. Tiffany hurried over and air kissed everyone, making certain her lipstick didn't accidentally end up where it shouldn't. Emersyn introduced Harvey to everyone as her dear friend.

With fifteen minutes to go, the rest of the staff from both Happy Girl and Chalmers and Tran that were invited to the event arrived, and Emersyn asked the band to put on some background music. With nothing else to do but wait, Emersyn found her eyes continually moving to the door in anticipation of the first guests arriving—or that's what she was telling herself. What she was truly doing was waiting for Arlo. Not that she had a clue what she would do once he was there.

Someone handed her a glass of the pink punch and she sipped on it, determined not to drink like she had at the last party she had thrown. Tonight, she would remain sober and able to take off her own shoes at the end of the night.

Emersyn looked around the room and was pleased with what she saw. She was extremely grateful to Matilda for allowing her this opportunity to continue to take the reins when it came to helping with the setup of this event. As the head of accounts, it really wasn't Emersyn's place to have anything to do with this but she had started with the ad campaign. It was her initial idea of the love hearts on the shower screens that had given Arlo the inspiration for the ads. And Emersyn felt close to it.

As the party began and people arrived, Emersyn took a step back; it was time for her to blend back into the shadows of what she did. This was not her moment nor her job. She took another glass of punch, and another one for Harvey, who looked uncomfortable standing there in his tailored suit that she had insisted on purchasing for him the day before. "Here." She handed him the glass.

"Thank you, Miss Emersyn. I must say this is delicious."

She held up her glass and clinked it against his. "To you, Harvey. I am not sure I could have come through everything without your unwavering support."

Harvey opened his mouth to speak but they were interrupted by Jaya. "Hey, Harvey, feeling brave?" she asked and gave him a huge grin.

"What exactly did you have in mind?"

"It's time to get this party going. Come and join me on the dance floor?" Jaya asked, and it almost sounded like begging. "Come on, I think you are hiding some excellent moves under that stuffy suit Emmy insisted you wear."

"Hey," Emersyn protested, "If he had his way, he would be wearing his uniform."

Jaya and Harvey laughed.

"Come on, let's dance," Jaya pleaded.

Harvey raised a heavy brow at her, and to Emersyn's surprise, drained the drink she had just handed him before handing her back the empty glass. "Why not? It's a new year, after all."

Jaya whooped in a very unladylike manner, causing several party goers to laugh, and took the older man's hand and hauled him to the neon pink dance floor. Emersyn watched them for a few moments, and just like at most parties, once someone took to the dance floor it encouraged others to join. She moved to the side of the room, pretending to find someone to take Harvey's empty glass as a reason to not stop chat. Her stomach was in knots as she reminded herself to not watch the door. *It's over,* she told herself as she took a moment to tidy up one of the gift areas, as the model giving out the goodies bag had needed to duck to the restroom, and Emersyn had been happy to oblige in manning the station. *If he wanted to say sorry or ask what had happened, he would have rung; he would have made the effort,* she told herself, just like she had for the past few weeks.

"What are you doing?" Jaya asked, her eyes narrowed at Emersyn.

"I'm helping."

"Hiding is more the word you are looking for."

"Very funny."

"Wasn't trying to be."

The model returned and thanked Emersyn for helping out. "See, I am helping." She smiled pointedly at Jaya.

"Mmmm, fine, but no more helping. I want photos together. Let's go." She linked her arm through Emersyn's and steered her towards the pretend shower stalls on the opposite wall.

They found an empty booth and spent the next ten minutes laughing hysterically and shrieking like school girls as they draped each other in hilarious looking props. It was good to stop thinking and just enjoy her friend's company. Jaya always managed to lift her spirits and find the joy in life. Emersyn was going to miss Jaya when she returned to New York in two days.

"You go wait for the photos to be developed, I don't want others seeing those shots, and I'll clean up all this." Emersyn indicated the pile of sunglasses, hats, feather boas, and the signs they had used in their photos.

"You worry too much about what other people think. People will see those photos and think 'look at those two women having fun,' and the ones that will judge aren't worth caring about anyway."

"You're right, but I also think this is a work function in essence and we have to be aware of that."

Jaya rolled her eyes. "Fine, be sensible." She finished by throwing her a wink and exiting the booth dramatically.

Emersyn sang softly to herself as she tidied the booth. She took her time to make certain everything looked perfect for the next people to use. The song she had been singing finished, and the booth filled with the sounds of the party as she heard the sound of the curtain open behind her. "How did the photos turn out?" she asked as she hung the tiara on its assigned hook.

Jaya didn't respond. *Probably got distracted, or didn't hear me. It is quite noisy in here*, she thought to herself. With everything in place, she turned to look at the photos and gasped as she was met by the glorious eyes of Arlo. He was too close. Her heart hammered in her chest and her stomach flipped flopped with butterflies and desire. Without thinking, Emersyn backed up, which allowed him to enter the booth completely and drop the curtain he had been holding.

"Hi." His smile was hesitant, soft, and real; not his usual cocky grin. It was the smile she remembered when she tortured herself by reliving that wonderful night together before it had fallen apart and he had run rather than talked. *Didn't you do the same thing?* her mind asked her. *Shut up*, she told herself.

—◇—

Arlo

His shirt collar felt too tight and his mouth full of cotton balls as Arlo struggled to find any words to say to the beautiful woman in front of him. She was perfect. Her emerald green eyes flashed with too many emotions for him to read at once, and he almost went to step backwards so she could leave, if she chose, when she took her own step backwards giving him space to enter the photo booth fully and drop the curtain. "Hi," was all he could think of to say.

Her eyes widened and he smiled shyly. Arlo could feel the electricity between them. It had always been there, but now it was heightened. It was if now his body had known hers it was all that it craved. But yet, it was more. Even though he longed to close the distance between them and kiss her passionately, he also longed to simply hold her, tell her he loved her, ask her what she had been doing, and what she was thinking. He wanted to know her on every level. It was terrifying and something he longed for.

"I missed you." He said the words he never thought he would say to a woman.

Emersyn responded with a short snort of derision. "You got a funny way of showing it."

Arlo frowned. "What do you mean?"

"Going on air and flirting with Felicity for the world to see."

Typically, he would have laughed at such a comment, but he got the feeling this was not the time to be dismissive. "That was not my intention. I wanted to be friendly and relaxed, but not flirtatious. I want to always be seen as professional."

She blinked at him but didn't answer.

"I think all of the phone calls I made but you didn't answer prove that I missed you."

"Phone calls?" Emersyn frowned at him. "What phone calls?"

The photo booth curtain swung open and they were greeted by a high-pitched squeal. "Oh my god, you came!" shouted Tiffany. She engulfed him in a hug.

"Yes, I needed to come and make things right."

"I did hear that you came to the office today and had a meeting with Dad. Though, between you and me, Pascal was a cow and you had nothing to apologize for."

Arlo couldn't help it, he laughed. "No, really, I needed to own my lapse in judgment."

The band began to play a new song and Tiffany again squealed. "I love this song. You can make up your lapse of judgment to me by joining me on the dance floor."

Arlo looked over her shoulder at the group of women standing behind Tiffany. "Um, aren't you supposed to be getting a photo?"

"You don't mind if I just squeeze in a quick dance before a photo, girls?" she asked.

"Of course not."

"No, go ahead."

"He's hot. Go dance."

Tiffany wiggled her eyebrows at him. "See, all happy to wait." She turned her head to Emersyn who had not spoken.

"You don't mind, do you, Emersyn?"

"He's all yours." Emersyn's smile was tight, but her words were light.

"Great. See, no excuses."

Before Arlo could protest further, Tiffany tugged his hand and dragged him out of the booth and away from Emersyn. But he did the right thing and danced with the young lady who had trusted him with this campaign and had helped to fix the mess he had made by sleeping with Pascal. After all, this was a launch party, and he was there to represent his firm. He danced with her for three more songs before he felt he could excuse himself from the dance floor, and by that time Emersyn had disappeared into the crowd.

He pushed his want to spend time with Emersyn and to tell her how he felt aside and spent the next hour catching up with Matilda and Jaya, as well as joining Tiffany on the dance floor with her friends.

It was nearing midnight and it was a calculated risk, but Arlo began to look earnestly for Emersyn. Maybe if he was close to her at midnight she would be more receptive to a celebratory kiss or at least a hug. He had never been drawn to someone like he was to her, and he couldn't ignore his desire.

Arlo eventually found her standing quietly in a corner talking to a man that he recognized as her butler, Harvey, and an older woman he had never seen before. Slowly, he wound his way through the excited crowd, and as he finally got clear of everyone, he stopped in his tracks as he watched the handsome, tall, dark man that Emersyn had caught up with last time they were in LA sneak up from behind and pick her up and swing her in a circle. "Sorry, babe, the last party took longer than I expected." Arlo caught the words as the music died and the band announced it was time to start counting down.

"Shit," Arlo muttered to himself as his plan evaporated.

Jaya came to stand beside him. "Ready for a fresh start?" she asked.

"Sorry?"

"New year, new start?"

He couldn't help it, he looked to Emersyn. "I was hoping on a fresh start."

"They're just friends." She rubbed her temples as she spoke.

The countdown had hit ten and it was too loud to do anything other than join in the counting. As the crowd shouted out "Happy New Year," Arlo wished his friend and former second-in-charge a happy new year and gave her a firm hug. He really did miss Jaya and her astute observations, as well as her strong work ethic and fun attitude. As he let her go, she swayed a little. "You okay?"

Jaya covered her mouth, but a large burp escaped. "No, I think I need to go. Not a good look to be sick at a work event, no matter if it's New Year."

"Here." He offered his arm. "Hold on and let's go speak to Emersyn."

They approached the quartet who were standing to the side. To avoid any awkwardness, Arlo got straight to the point. "Jaya isn't feeling well; she's got a headache."

Harvey spoke first. "I will make sure Miss Jaya gets home."

"No, no, you stay," Emersyn interrupted. She looked meaningfully at the pretty woman standing at his side. "I am certain Anne will need someone to see her home. I can take Jaya home."

"Shouldn't you be here until the end?" Emersyn's male friend interjected.

Arlo kept his face neutral. "It's fine. I am happy to take Jaya home. As long as your *friend* here is okay seeing you safely home, Emmy?" Arlo put an emphasis on friend.

"Jaya, you good if Arlo takes you home?"

"Yeah, you should stay. Arlo will get me back to your place and make sure I am taken care of."

Emersyn turned to her friend. "How did you get here?"

"I drove. Didn't want to risk missing out on kissing you on New Year by waiting for a taxi."

She blushed but didn't comment. Arlo ground his back teeth together to stop himself from reacting to the comment.

"I've got a hired car here. I can drive Jaya wherever she needs to go," explained Arlo.

"Great." Emersyn's smile grew wide and it made Arlo's heart hurt. "That leaves the limo and driver to you, Harvey. He's on the clock till dawn, so have fun."

Arlo felt Jaya's grip tighten on his forearm and she swayed against him. "Okay, it's all settled. Have a good rest of your night."

And with that, he gently guided his friend out of the party, ignoring his need to look over his shoulder to see if Emersyn was watching.

Chapter 37

Arlo

Jaya's snoring reverberated around the luxurious lounge, making Arlo smile as he walked into the room with two steaming cups of coffee in his hands. He had been gone several minutes making coffee, and by the time he had got back, Jaya was sprawled on the expensive oversized white lounge. There was a throw rug placed artfully over one of the sofas and Arlo picked it up and carefully laid it over the passed out form of his friend. He picked up his mug and stood looking at the huge painting that hung on the wall above the faux fireplace.

A stunning painting of a young woman with green eyes and auburn hair, smiling down at her green-eyed daughter with pure love. It was all done in muted tones of white and gold with only the hair and eye color standing out. It did not take much imagination to realize this was a portrait of Emersyn and her mother. His heart ached for the woman he loved. To lose your mother so young was a tragedy.

He sipped his coffee and looked at the gorgeous white Christmas tree standing in front of the window, filled with gold ornaments that glittered in the moonlight that shone through. It was so very different from the one that sat in his parents' front window. Theirs was full of a riot of colored baubles as well as paper chains that the family made every year—this year there had been silver and green reindeer stamped on the paper. It was lopsided and chaotic but still as beautiful.

This mansion had a completely different aesthetic, and he wasn't sure if he liked it. While opulent and breath taking with its brilliant white furniture, stark white marble floors, and yellow-gold trimming everywhere, Arlo didn't feel the same warmth as he had in the Austin place. He wondered if there was a picnic tree in the back of this place too.

Arlo finished his coffee and took his empty mug, plus Jaya's now-cold-but-still-full cup into the kitchen to wash and put away. He didn't need Harvey angry with him by messing up his kitchen.

After making sure everything was back in its proper place, Arlo returned to the snoring Jaya and flicked off the light, plunging the room into darkness. Soon his eyes adjusted to the lack of light and he settled into a large armchair that looked out into the driveway. He didn't mean to, but he must have dozed off because the next thing he knew he was woken by the sound of car tires on the gravel driveway. He looked at his watch, it was after 2:00 a.m. He growled but tried to push any possessive thoughts down. She was a grown woman and could get home whenever she liked.

His growling must have disturbed Jaya because her voice filled the air. "Who's there?"

"It's Arlo. Sorry, I didn't mean to wake you. You fell asleep on the couch and I wasn't about to carry you around looking for the right bedroom."

"Yes, there has been enough misunderstandings already, let's not add to them," she said cryptically.

"What's that supposed to mean?"

A car door interrupted her answer. "Is that what you were growling at?" The bright moonlight clearly showed Jeremy walking around and opening the door for Emersyn.

He chose not to comment.

"Ah, I see. We are still pretending we don't care."

They both watched as Emersyn took Jeremy's proffered hand and before she could let go, the handsome man pulled her into his arms and kissed her firmly on the mouth. Arlo turned away. "Friend, indeed," he muttered. "I'm out of here."

Without any further talk, he headed for the back door; he had no intention of confronting anyone now he knew the truth. What an absolute fool he had been. He had never wanted to cry so badly. If this is what being in love was then he didn't want any part of it. Meaningless dating and sex was a far safer option for his heart and soul. Arlo only hoped that by the time he had made it round to the front of the house, Jeremy and Emersyn had moved inside and he didn't have to witness anything else.

—◇—

Emersyn

Jeremy had his arms around her and his lips pressed against hers before she knew what was happening. It took a few moments for her brain to catch up, but once it did, Emersyn responded by breaking the kiss and taking a step back. "Jeremy, no," she breathed.

"I thought I felt a connection. We've been hanging out so much." Jeremy put his hands up and looked alarmed. "I am so sorry. I hope this doesn't affect our friendship. I won't do it again."

"I am sorry, Jeremy, I just don't think of you like that."

"It's that guy, isn't it?"

"What guy?" Emmy acted like she had no clue who he spoke of.

He just laughed at her and ran his fingers over his tight black curls. "Okay, be that way."

"Thanks for driving me home." She changed the topic.

"No problem." He walked back around to his door. "No hard feelings about the kiss, right?"

"It's fine, just don't do it again. If I want you to kiss me I will ask you to."

"Got it." Jeremy didn't say anything further, he just got into the car, backed up a bit, and then drove away. It was only then did Emersyn see the other car parked in the cover of darkness near her garage. Was Arlo still here? Of course he was. He wouldn't leave Jaya, who was sick, by herself. He was a good friend.

Emersyn hurried as quickly as she could to the front door, the high stiletto heels and gravel was a lethal combination, and she didn't want to twist an ankle. She paused to gather her thoughts. Emersyn didn't want to appear too eager when she went through the door; after all, she was still furious at him. The hypocrisy of the moment was not lost on her. Emersyn moved to open the door only to have it opened for her. It was Jaya. Emersyn tried not to show her disappointment. "You feeling any better?"

Jaya moved back into the house. "Yes, much better. Had a little nap on the couch, and only woke when you pulled into the driveway."

Emersyn followed her into the lounge, noticing Arlo wasn't there. "Oh, sorry."

"Nothing to be sorry about, though we did get to witness your goodnight kiss."

"We?" Panic fluttered in her stomach.

"Yes, *we*." Jaya sat down and looked up at her. "He left."

Emersyn's stomach twisted and her chest tightened. "I wish he would stop running every time something happens. He never gives me a chance to explain."

"Okay, I'm here. What do you want to explain?" Arlo's voice filled the room.

Emersyn spun to find Arlo, arms crossed over his chest and a scowl on his handsome face. Her instinct was to run to him and kiss him, but her damaged heart stopped her. She couldn't handle any further rejection. "You came back," she whispered, astonished to see him.

"Yes, I don't want to be that guy anymore." He unfolded his arms.

"What type of guy do you want to be?" Her voice was small.

"The kind that stays and works on things when they get difficult, and to show my vulnerability." He took a step toward her. "The type that makes his woman always feel like she comes first." He took another step and Emersyn was reminded of him stalking up the stairs toward her while she backed away. This time she held her ground; there would be no running for her either. "A man who shows his fear and accepts his woman's comfort."

It was then that Emersyn saw the fear in his brown eyes, and she realized how much he was revealing of himself even though he still didn't know if she had returned Jeremy's kiss. She put her own fears of betrayal aside and took a step toward him—she needed to meet him halfway. "I want to give comfort and receive it. I want to find a safe space to be me and not fear that my man is bedding other women." Her eyes searched his, all her defenses down. "Can you honestly be that man? Can you give up the women, the conquest?" She held her breath.

"Emmy, who was the woman and child in the lobby?" He now stood in front of her.

Emersyn swallowed hard. She knew Jaya was still in the room, but it was time to stop holding onto the pain and embarrassment of the past. These two were in her corner and she had to open her heart and trust. It was now or never. "The woman is Samantha Huffington and the child is Sahara, the daughter of Samantha and my ex-husband, Nikolai. It turns out he liked to always have a woman on the side.

Pretty, rich socialites, looking for a thrill. This one just happened to fall pregnant, and when Nikolai wouldn't marry her, she told me about all the women and her child in the hope it would force his hand. I did leave him, but he refused to marry her still. He has told her he can't pay her more child support because I took all his money so she came to Austin, to blackmail me into giving her the money she thinks I took. The first contact for money she made was while we were in LA." Emersyn's voice was dull, much like the ache talking about those days made her feel. It was a relief to realize she could talk about it and not have her voice catch or tears well up.

"The night I screwed everything up the first time?" Arlo guessed.

She smiled at his admission of it being the first time he screwed up. "Yes."

"And then I acted like a child when you got offered a job, and the next day Samantha turns up." Arlo blew out a deep breath. "I am an idiot. No wonder you behaved oddly."

"Yes, you are an idiot."

All three in the room laughed, which broke the tension. Jaya then cleared her throat as she stood up from the couch and came towards them. "Thank you for sharing that with me." She gave Emersyn a hug. "I am going to bed." She released Emersyn. Jaya stood back and gave them both a stern look. "Neither of you leave this room until all the words are spoken." And with that parting piece of advice, Jaya flicked her dark hair over her shoulder and left them.

Arlo took Emersyn's hand. "That morning in the lobby, I was waiting for you to apologize for being a jerk about the job offer when you suddenly changed back into the distant you, pushing me into the elevator, away from you. I got up to my office to find out my mother had been calling. Papa had been diagnosed with cancer—" His voice paused for a moment and Emersyn squeezed his hand.

"Oh, Arlo, I am sorry. I wish you had told me. I wish I could have been there for you."

He lifted his other hand and cupped her cheek. "Thank you." Arlo lowered his head to hers and softly kissed her.

Emersyn's heart exploded as their lips met. She had been hoping for this moment for so long. He pulled back from her and she almost whimpered at the loss of contact. "Is your Papa okay?" she asked, remembering there was more important things than her lust.

"Yes. I am sorry I left like that though. I should have come to your office and told you what was happening, not just run away from all my emotions."

"I wish you would have." She frowned and pulled away, remembering the months of pain he had caused. "I am glad your Papa is fine." She went to sit on the couch, her thoughts confused, and she needed distance from him to think clearly.

Arlo followed her. "What just happened? You've grown distant again."

"It has been months since then. If you really cared, you would have reached out. You would have contacted me to tell me what had happened and to apologize."

He sat still. "I tried to pretend for a while that I didn't care, that it had been all in my head. It wasn't until I was home for Christmas and I talked to my Papa that I came to terms with that fact that I was avoiding you and the situation because I was scared of getting hurt, of putting everything out there and finding out I wasn't enough. I told you at the party I have been trying to ring you for days to tell you, but you never answered. Why didn't you answer?" His voice sounded desperate.

Emersyn frowned. "I haven't received a single phone call from you."

"But I called, again and again and again."

Understanding finally dawned on her and she began to laugh. "I lost my phone and had to get a new one. I couldn't get the same number. A memo was sent around, I am sure."

"I wonder why I didn't get the memo."

Emersyn had a suspicion about a certain secretary in the Austin office who may have deliberately neglected to CC him into the email. She had no proof, just a gut feeling she had come to trust, but chose not to say nothing, as what was the point?

"Seriously?"

"Yes, seriously."

"So, you haven't been ignoring me?"

"No."

"Would you have answered if the calls did come through?" he asked her pointedly.

She closed her eyes for a second and then opened them to look out onto the moonlit driveway. "I really don't know. You hurt me, and I am tired of being disappointed and abandoned when things get hard. First it was my father, then Nikolai, and now you. Harvey is the only male that has shown me how good and kind and loyal men can be."

"What about Jeremy?"

Emersyn turned back to Arlo and placed both of her hands on his shoulders. "He is a friend, has only ever been a friend, and will only ever be a friend. He kissed me tonight, but as soon as I said no, he stopped."

"Okay."

"Okay?" She paused. "That's it?"

"Yes, I trust you." He moved his face closer to hers. "And I am going to spend the rest of our lives earning and keeping your trust. There is no one else for me, Emmy. I love you."

Emersyn saw the truth behind his words, and in that moment her heart became whole, and she knew whatever the future brought she would be cherished. "I love you, Arlo."

Epilogue

Arlo

Arlo stretched out in the magnificent king-sized bed. They had been together a year and he still couldn't believe the luxury in which he found himself. He lay still and listened to Emmy making sounds in the bathroom while she quietly sang to herself. Arlo smiled and silently thanked the universe for allowing him the chance to spend eternity with the stunning woman on the other side of the bathroom doors.

The first few months together had been difficult and beautiful for both of them as he learned more of her ex-husband's betrayal and got her to understand he was many things but never a cheater. In turn, she showed him what love could look like if he just stopped worrying about what he thought it should look like. It had been a time for adjustments as they had a long distance relationship for six months. That is until Chalmers and Tran finally agreed the best fit for the company would be for Arlo to move out to LA as the other guy they had hired was good, but hadn't hit the ground running like they had hoped.

Arlo heard the shower turn on and counted to five before he tossed the bedsheets aside and pulled on a pair of shorts. He opened his bedside table drawer and took out a velvet box and moved to open the bathroom doors. What he found made him grin.

Emersyn stood with her hands over her mouth, her eyes wide, as she looked at the love heart that had formed on the glass screen as the heated water steamed up the shower. Words were appearing as the mist grew. Within the love heart, the words "marry me" materialized.

Her eyes moved to his face as he walked to the shower edge and dropped to one knee on the tiled floor. He snapped the box open to reveal an exquisite two-carat emerald cut diamond, with sparkling dark baguette-cut emeralds on either side, tapering in length. All within a platinum setting.

"Emmy, you make me happy in every way. Will you marry me?"

Arlo watched as a slow smile spread across her full lips and she moved out of the shower. "Yes. I will marry you."

He stood and took the ring out and carefully slipped it onto her finger. It fit perfectly. Arlo pulled her to him and kissed her, sealing the proposal. As they broke apart, they both looked to the large love heart that had not disappeared from the shower screen. "How did you do that?" she asked.

"I channeled my inner teen boy and realized he would have done it with candle wax."

They both laughed at the inside joke before she pulled him into the shower.

———◇———

Emersyn

The tree with its limbs splayed out in all directions, as if trying to grasp everything at once, gave them enough shade that their naked bodies wouldn't burn in the blazing sun of another LA summer. They had been enjoying a picnic under the tree as a final goodbye to the house before they moved to London the following day to open

Chalmers and Tran's first international office. Harvey had left the week before with his new wife to set up everything for their arrival. The cleaning crew was due tomorrow, once they handed their keys over to Jeremy who would rent the mansion out. Emersyn couldn't bring herself to sell it, even though she had sold many of the other houses she had inherited when her father had succumbed to his alcoholism the year before.

Emersyn and Arlo were truly alone and had taken advantage of the moment by taking the afternoon to swim naked in the pool and laze under the tree without thought of embarrassing any of the household staff. Emersyn panted as her core clamped down on the two fingers Arlo had inside her, the palm of his hand rubbed against her in a steady circle. His teeth bit softly down on her nipple and she arched her back as her hand twisted in the picnic blanket beneath her. He withdrew his fingers and she whimpered as she hung there so close to the edge of her orgasm. Arlo pulled her onto her side to face him and brought her top leg up over his hip. Without a word, he pushed into her and she gasped with pleasure. Her body responded to his touch and she leaned back, his hands on her hips, keeping her still as he moved into her while he bent forward, his mouth sought her breasts.

She let the moment carry her away. Arlo was her everything, and their joining was perfect as they raced to their combined orgasm. Emersyn clawed his perfect ass with one hand, her other arm she laid on was under his head and she moved it so she could grab his hair. He trailed his kisses up her chest and onto her neck before kissing her deeply. "I love you, Emmy," he gasped as his body stiffened next to her.

Emersyn's body responded and she too tumbled over the edge with a limb-shattering orgasm. She felt herself contract around him, making him respond with a grunt and another quiver. Emersyn grinned as she did it again, this time on purpose, tightening her internal muscles.

It was wicked and fun to see him shiver. He kissed her and whispered, "You are magnificent."

"I love you," she said as she settled closer to him—she didn't want him to leave her yet.

"Emmy, are you truly okay with leaving here?"

She pulled back and looked into his gold-flecked brown eyes. "I am. These three years have been wonderful, but I am looking forward to starting over with you. New city, new office, new house—" She paused before she said the next words. "New baby."

"Mmm," he murmured as she watched his face change as understanding dawned. "New baby?"

"Yes, a baby." She laughed.

He pulled her to him and kissed her. "You will be an amazing mother."

She returned his kiss. "And you will be a loving Papa."

"Now we will have to find the ideal house with the one thing every child should have," Arlo announced as he cupped her face and kissed her nose.

"And what is that?"

"The perfect picnic spot."

Romantic Women's Fiction

Reflections of Love Collection
Also releasing on Radish and available in Audio format

Hannah

Samantha

Olivia

Chloe

Lacy

Grace

Reflections of Love Novella Collection Volume 1 (Contains books 1 – 4)

For more information on all titles head to tayarune.com

About Taya Rune

Taya Rune is a writer of romance, a sucker for happy endings, and has a knack for asking people uncomfortable questions.

She is a USA Today Bestselling Author and a finalist for the 2022 Romantic Book of the Year, for the Romance Writer's of Australia RuBY awards. She has had her work published in many different anthologies and publications.

Acknowledgments

I would like to take a few moments
to say thank you.

To my children, thank you for
teaching me to let go of the small stuff. I am proud of you.

To my family, thank you for the
love and support you have shown me throughout the years.

To my friends, the ones that have
my back and are forever in my corner – I cherish you.

To my editor, Rochelle J. Simas – IDK art.
Thank you for the kind words that
always accompany the return of my fabulously edited manuscripts.

To my ARC, Street and Beta Teams.
You are appreciated.

Newsletter

To receive up-to-date information, news and exclusive offers online
please sign up for the
Taya Rune newsletter.

https://www.tayarune.com/subscribe

Follow her on your favorite platform:

Website:

https://www.tayarune.com

Facebook:

https://www.facebook.com/taya.rune.75

Facebook Group:

https://www.facebook.com/groups/tayasromanticrealm

Instagram:

https://www.instagram.com/tayarune/

Twitter:

https://twitter.com/TayaRune

Bookbub:

https://www.bookbub.com/authors/taya-rune

Goodreads:

https://www.goodreads.com/author/show/21156065.Taya_Rune

TikTok:

https://www.tiktok.com/@tayarune

Pinterest:

https://www.pinterest.com.au/TayaRune

Taya Rune